Dr. Fell and the Playground of DOOM

Dr. Fell and the Playground of DOOM

DAVID NEILSEN

CROWN BOOKS
FOR YOUNG READERS
NEW YORK

This book is dedicated
to children with
the curiosity to
peer into the darkness.

 Published in the United States by Crown Books for Young Readers, an imprint of Random House Children's Books, a division of Penguin Random House LLC, New York.

Crown and the colophon are registered trademarks of Penguin Random House LLC.

Visit us on the Web! randomhousekids.com

Educators and librarians, for a variety of teaching tools, visit us at RHTeachersLibrarians.com

Library of Congress Cataloging-in-Publication Data
Neilsen, David.
Dr. Fell and the playground of doom / David Neilsen. — First edition.
pages cm
Summary: "Three children must defeat a mysterious doctor who builds an irresistible and dangerous playground in their neighborhood and then uses his power to heal children who get injured—stealing some of their life essence in the process"—Provided by publisher.
ISBN 978-1-101-93578-1 (trade) — ISBN 978-1-101-93579-8 (lib. bdg.) —
ISBN 978-1-101-93580-4 (ebook)
[1. Good and evil—Fiction. 2. Supernatural—Fiction. 3. Neighborhoods—Fiction.] I. Title.
II. Title: Doctor Fell and the playground of doom.
PZ7.1.N4Dr 2016 [Fic]—dc23 2015017787

Printed in the United States of America
10 9 8 7 6 5 4 3 2 1
First Edition

Random House Children's Books supports the
First Amendment and celebrates the right to read.

I do not like thee, Doctor Fell,
The reason why I cannot tell;
But this I know, and know full well,
I do not like thee, Doctor Fell.

—Tom Brown, 1680

Contents

Chapter 1

The Arrival of Dr. Fell

THE LARGE BRICK HOUSE at the end of Hardscrabble Street had been empty for a generation. During that time it had been a royal castle, a haunted ruin, an alien spaceship, and anything else the children of the neighborhood wanted it to be.

Lindsey Brackentwig said the last people to live in the house had been a family of circus performers who had practiced their skills on the abnormally flat roof. Josh Gallowsbee said they had been three witches who had stirred magic potions in the enormous bathtub on the second floor. Hannah Festerworth said they had been the parents of a young boy whom they kept locked away in the unfinished basement.

Every child had a story about the house, each wilder than the last. It was a house of imagination, a blank canvas just waiting to be painted with the gleeful brushstrokes of youth. Every parent in the neighborhood had forbidden their children from entering the house, and every parent in the neighborhood knew full well their children were disobeying them.

But when local real estate agent Dorothy Canvaswalter placed a Sold banner atop the aged, weather-beaten For Sale sign that had stood sentry on the front lawn for years, even the parents were disappointed.

"It's like the heart of the neighborhood is being ripped right out," said PTA Co-President Candice Gloomfellow.

"I still remember when little Johnny broke his arm falling down those rickety stairs," agreed PTA Co-President Martha Doomburg with a wistful tear in her eye.

Every adult on Hardscrabble Street, as well as all those on nearby Vexington Avenue and Von Burden Lane, and nearly all on Turnabout Road (Old Lady Witherton could not be bothered), wondered about the new owners. Would they be a tidy family? Would they be a handy family? Would they be a noisy family?

The children of Hardscrabble Street, Vexington Avenue, Von Burden Lane, and Turnabout Road did not wonder about the new owners. As word spread of the sale, they gathered in twos and threes to stand in front of their magnificent former playhouse and sigh, pout, even weep. Some felt childhood was over. Others felt they had lost their best friend. All felt mildly resentful of the sale and were determined to dislike whoever ultimately moved in, no matter what.

"Why would anyone buy that house?" asked ten-year-old Gail Bloom, staring longingly at a second-floor balcony on which she'd fenced the imaginary-yet-dastardly Lord Dunderhead only days before.

"Maybe they've got kids," answered her eight-year-old brother, Jerry, with his rose-colored viewpoint, eyeing the flat roof where only last week he'd set up his slot-car track and raced the cars wildly in circles for hours on end. "This is a good neighborhood for kids."

"But it's our place," complained Gail's best friend and Jerry's worst nightmare, ten-year-old Nancy Pinkblossom, imagining the infamous Stairway of Death down which she'd tumbled each and every one of her Pretty Patty dress-up dolls. "Who said they could just come and take it away from us?"

The three children stood in place a moment more on that warm spring Saturday morning—each gathering and storing away an admittedly short lifetime's worth of memories. Finally, at some unspoken signal, they turned away almost in unison.

"What should we do today?" asked Gail.

"We could go to the river," answered Jerry, referring to the tiny trickle of a stream that snaked behind Hardscrabble Street. "There's lots to do near the river."

"She wasn't asking you, Snothead," said Nancy automatically, too upset to muster up a real insult.

"Wanna go see if Lindsey Brackentwig's home?" suggested Gail.

"Sure," said Jerry. "She's fun."

"Go find your own friends, Dorknose," said Nancy.

"I'm not a dorknose."

"Yes, you are. You're a total dorknose."

"You're a dorknose."

"Oh God, grow up, Dorknose."

"Guys, who's that?" interrupted Gail.

Jerry and Nancy put their epic Battle of the Dorknose on hold to follow the line of Gail's finger to a tall, frail-looking man shambling toward them, hunched over as if he had long ago lost the struggle against gravity. He was dressed all in black except for a huge purple top hat, and he carried a small black leather bag by its polished white handle of bone. Even though he was still a ways away, the kids could make out a repeated creaking that sounded with each footstep, as if he were walking on a squeaky wooden floor rather than a concrete sidewalk.

The children stared at the strange man as he approached, and he at them. But where the children gawked in open-mouthed wonder, the man merely smiled.

"A supremely pleasant good morning to you, urchins," announced the man slowly in a high-pitched, weak, warbling voice. "Are you residents of this fine enclave of humanity?"

The children remained slack-jawed a moment more until the man chuckled good-naturedly.

"Forgive my manner of speech, young ones. What I mean to say is . . . do you live here?"

Gail and Nancy remained immobile, but Jerry managed to nod slightly.

A wide grin forced its way across the thin, heavily wrinkled face. "Then I am delighted to make your acquaintance. My name is Dr. Fell. How do you do?"

Dr. Fell extended a pale, bony hand toward the children. They watched it approach as if it were in slow motion, each knobby knuckle looking like it was ready to crack into dust at the faintest breeze. Finally, Gail, not wanting to be impolite, met the hand with her own and gave it a limp shake, careful not to exert too much pressure for fear of crushing the old man's fingers.

"Hi" was all she said.

"I've just purchased the very house you stand before," wheezed Dr. Fell. "I'm your new neighbor."

The children looked the man up and down. Gail, who had released the hand, wondered why such an elderly individual would choose to move into this loud and boisterous community so late in life. Jerry tried to imagine the decrepit figure climbing up and down the Stairway of Death each day without breaking a leg.

Nancy, however, got right to point. "That was our playhouse."

Dr. Fell raised first one eyebrow, then the other, before looking out over the heads of the children at his new home. "Was it? How dreadfully rude of me," he said, then smiled back down at Nancy. "I do apologize. I trust this will not forever damage our relationship?"

Nancy, who normally would stand toe to toe with anybody, felt the need to take a step back, bumping into Gail, who gently nudged her aside.

"What she means, sir—" began Gail.

"Please," interrupted Dr. Fell. "I'm not a sir. Heaven knows I've not been knighted. I am simply Dr. Fell." As he spoke his name, he bowed his already-bowed body even more. There was a sudden flash of sunlight as something shiny slipped out of his jacket pocket and clattered to the ground at his feet.

"Oh!" cried Dr. Fell in alarm.

"I got it," said Jerry, quickly stooping to pick it up. He moved to hand it to the old man but stopped when he saw what it was—a gold pocket watch.

"Thank you, young sir, for retrieving my little trinket," said Dr. Fell. "I'll take that now."

Wordlessly, Jerry handed the watch back, and Dr. Fell carefully tucked it into his pocket. "Now then," he continued, "you were in the midst of explaining how my recent real-estate purchase had upset the unwashed masses."

"Well," continued Gail, "your house has sort of been the unofficial playground for the neighborhood as long as any of us can remember."

An odd, mute understanding slowly dawned on the face of Dr. Fell. "Oh, my dear bones. I imagine there are quite a number of disappointed young urchins hereabouts due to my arrival." He looked back at the house, his eyes seeming to focus inward for a moment. "I shall have to find a means of making amends."

Despite his pleasant words, friendly smile, and easygoing nature, something about Dr. Fell gave all three children the briefest of shivers on that warm spring Saturday morning.

"Indeed," continued the good doctor. "That will be paramount."

Jerry tugged on his sister's arm. "Come on—let's go to Lindsey's house," he said.

"Yeah," said Nancy, happily going along with the lie. "She's waiting for us."

"Running along, are you?" asked Dr. Fell. "Well, it has been an absolute pleasure to meet you. Do have yourselves a festive and fantastically fun day."

He jerked his hand up toward his purple top hat, struggling to lift his arm above his shoulders. Finally, his shaking fingers reached the hat's brim, and gripping it tightly, he tilted both his hat and head slightly downward in farewell. "I'm sure I'll be seeing each of you again soon enough."

The children ran all the way to Lindsey Brackentwig's house.

Chapter 2

The Speculation over Dr. Fell

THE MOVING VANS ARRIVED the next day.

There were a great many of them, and they took turns backing into the driveway, unloading their contents, and driving away. Each van was filled to the point of bursting with furniture, boxes, racks of clothing, more furniture, more boxes, and quite a few very large and very mysterious wooden crates.

It was this parade of crates that became the favored subject of gossip all Sunday long. Lars Oozewuld, who had stopped for a breather in front of Dr. Fell's house while taking the Oozewuld family Pomeranian for a walk, swore to Nathan Festerworth that he'd heard eerie scratching noises coming from within one of the crates. Sandy Gallowsbee, who had chosen to take her daily speed walk up and down Hardscrabble Street rather than along her usual haunt of Von Burden Lane, told Veronica Plaugestein she'd seen dim, green smoke trail out of one of them. Edna Pusster, who had wandered into Dr. Fell's front yard in search of her son, Ethan (despite knowing full well he was at home watching television), let Monica Brackentwig know that she had smelled the undeniable scent of formaldehyde coming from another.

"He works for a foreign government, and those crates are filled with stolen zoo animals!" accused PTA Co-President Candice Gloomfellow.

"He works for our government, and those crates are filled with nuclear waste!" corrected PTA Co-President Martha Doomburg.

Every adult had a theory about the crates, each wilder than the last.

Dr. Fell, for his part, spent much of the afternoon standing on his shaded porch in his purple top hat nodding politely to the movers as they unloaded van after van, his bent and broken frame seemingly ever on the verge of toppling over. He didn't seem to be giving any directions, noticed Abner Fallowmold as he watched the action through his living room window, but the vans were emptied with clockwork precision. As if the movers already knew where everything needed to go.

The people of Hardscrabble Street, as well as the people of Vexington Avenue and Von Burden Lane and most of the people from Turnabout Road (Old Lady Witherton could not be bothered), spent most of the day trying to get a good look at Dr. Fell himself. It should have been a simple matter, seeing as how he spent the day on his porch. Yet none was able to form a satisfying image of the man in their mind. Certainly the purple top hat covered his hair, and his sleek black suit covered his body, but they would have thought that his face, which was not covered by anything, would have been easily observable despite the doctor's pronounced hunch. Yet no matter where they were (and they took turns spying on him from nearly every house on the street), there always seemed to be something blocking their view of Dr. Fell. A hanging plant. The porch railing. The shadow from his purple top hat. A surprisingly large housefly.

The movers, on the other hand, were easily seen, easily identified, and easily gossiped over. They were all bald. Van after van backed up Dr. Fell's driveway and spat out a team of bald men to unload more furniture, more boxes, and particularly more large, mysterious crates. And they weren't simply the same few bald men each time. There were tall bald men and short bald men, fat bald men and skinny bald men, young bald men and old bald men.

"They're all monks!" declared Horace Macabrador.

"They're all bowlers!" announced Sharon Rottingsly.

"They're all bald!" cried Jud Fetidsky, who had a habit of stating the obvious.

Finally, as the sun set, the last van pulled out of the driveway, drove down Hardscrabble Street, and disappeared into the evening dusk. Dr. Fell watched it go, then turned and gave a pleasant smile and shaky wave to the neighborhood before shuffling inside into the darkness of his waiting home.

McKinley Grant Fillmore Elementary School was all abuzz on Monday morning, as rumors about Dr. Fell were on every tongue and in every ear.

"He has a flying carpet!" guessed Crystal Chintzington.

"He drives a rocket car!" guessed Abby Goldbaum.

"He has three heads!" guessed Sam Blingforth, who had a rather uncontrollable imagination.

Children who happened to live anywhere near the suddenly famous Dr. Fell found themselves the center of attention. Most went to great lengths to prove they knew more about the good doctor than anyone else. Albert Rottingsly proudly told any who would listen that he was already on a first-name basis with Dr. Fell (though he wasn't able to say just what that first name was). Gabby Plaugestein gave an incredibly detailed and completely invented list of everything contained within the large mysterious crates. And Bud Fetidsky told everybody that the moving men had all been bald (he'd learned that from his father).

Two of the only three kids in the entire school who were *not* interested in Dr. Fell that day were Gail Bloom and Nancy Pinkblossom (Jerry Bloom being the third). As the girls sat together in the back of Mrs. Worth's fifth-grade class, Nancy didn't tell anyone about the way Dr. Fell's shoes squeaked when he walked on concrete, nor did Gail tell anyone about how fragile and brittle his bones had seemed beneath her fingers. Instead, they tried to concentrate on their schoolwork.

Unfortunately, Mrs. Worth was just as nosey as everyone else.

"Bloom! Pinkblossom! Don't the two of you live on Hardscrabble Street?" asked their teacher in the middle of a lecture on multiplying fractions.

"Um . . . yes. Yes, we do," answered Gail.

"So did you see Dr. Fell this weekend? What's he like? Is he really seven feet tall?"

Gail glanced at Nancy for help.

"We didn't really get a good look at him," said Nancy, lying with ease.

"Right—we spent most of the weekend playing by the river," agreed Gail, hoping the small fib wouldn't cause her cheeks to become overly red. Gail was not as good at lying as Nancy.

"Oh. That's a pity," said Mrs. Worth, who obviously felt it was much more than a pity. "I have an idea. When the two of you go home tonight, you should spend some time staring down the street at Dr. Fell's house."

Mrs. Worth's face lit up as she said this. "In fact, let's make that your homework. Don't worry about math or ELA or anything else. Just sit by your windows and watch Dr. Fell's house all night. In the morning, you can present your report to the class and tell us what you saw." She beamed, pleased with herself. "Yes, I think that's an excellent idea."

Everyone agreed that it was an excellent idea.

Everyone except Gail and Nancy.

Meanwhile, in Mrs. Wealthini's third-grade class, Jerry was having an equally difficult time avoiding talk of Dr. Fell. Mrs. Wealthini continually found ways to slip the subject into whatever she happened to be teaching at any particular moment.

"The water-holding frog of Australia's deserts burrows into the ground during the hot days of summer, much like this new Dr. Fell seems to be burrowing into his new home on Hardscrabble Street," said Mrs. Wealthini. "Meanwhile, the red-eyed tree frog has bulging eyes, much like the people who live on Hardscrabble Street must have had this weekend when they saw Dr. Fell move into that empty house."

So far, Jerry had managed to avoid telling anyone about his encounter with Dr. Fell, though that was mainly because very few people in the third grade were aware that he lived on Hardscrabble Street. To be honest, very few people in the third grade were aware of Jerry Bloom, period. This occasionally bothered Jerry, but today he was thankful. The last thing he wanted to do was admit to anyone that talking to Dr. Fell had made him feel so . . . so . . .

So uncomfortable.

So he kept his head down and waited for the day to end.

Chapter 3

The Gift of Dr. Fell

THERE WAS A SURPRISE waiting for the children of Hardscrabble Street when they returned home from school.

"Whoa," said Christian Gloomfellow.

"Check it out," said Johnny Doomburg.

"Dude!" said Zachary Fallowmold.

In front of Dr. Fell's house stood an enormous wooden structure. It had stairs and slides and poles and ladders and ropes and handholds and trapdoors and secret panels on multiple levels, with dozens of entrances and exits. From one angle, it resembled the most awesome pirate ship ever imagined, while from another, it was obviously a totally cool spaceship. From a third angle, it stood tall as a perfect medieval castle, while from a fourth, it beckoned to one and all as a post-apocalyptic, zombie-infested wasteland.

It was, in short, the greatest playhouse any girl or boy had ever seen in the entire history of girls and boys.

The children were drawn to it like flies to flypaper.

"This is awesome!" shouted a gleeful Albert Rottingsly, swinging from a rope.

"Best! Playground! Ever!" shouted a jubilant Gabby Plaugestein, scrambling up a climbing wall.

"I never want to leave!" shouted an enraptured Gore Oozewuld, leaping from platform to platform.

As the children played, frolicked, cavorted, and romped over every square inch of the wooden structure, Dr. Fell stood to one side in his near-horizontal position, smiling pleasantly from beneath his purple top hat and watching the children lose themselves in boundless joy on the magical construction that had sprung to life while they had toiled away at school.

"Where did that come from?" asked Gail as she, Nancy, and Jerry stepped off the school bus and caught sight of the playground.

"Who cares? It rocks!" shouted Josh Gallowsbee, brushing past the three of them and racing down the street to join in the revelry.

"That was not here this morning," stated Jerry.

"No, it wasn't," answered Nancy, before remembering to add, "Dorknose."

Curious, the three approached the massive structure, which now dominated the end of Hardscrabble Street. More

and more children raced past them to climb all over the Taj Mahal of playhouses, and the air was soon filled with peals of laughter and screams of rapture such as you would normally expect to hear only from children on a major sugar buzz.

There was some serious fun happening.

Gail, Nancy, and Jerry, however, ambled more hesitantly forward, not overcome with the same sense of frenzied jubilation as their peers.

"A supremely pleasant good afternoon to you, urchins," wheezed Dr. Fell as the three children walked up the driveway, their eyes focused laser-like on the playhouse. "Though I can never undo the inadvertent damage my arrival has done to the children of this fine neighborhood, I hope my humble offering of goodwill may begin to place me in a better light."

Each of them involuntarily took a few steps toward the scene of gleeful chaos before standing their ground. "Wow," said Jerry, unable to turn away.

Dr. Fell glowed at the praise. "I must thank the three of you for informing me the other day as to the nature of my grave offense," he said. "It allowed me to put my nose to the grindstone to work on a thorny issue I had not even known was facing me." Dr. Fell spoke the last words with as grand a sweep of his ancient arms as his aged body allowed. It was as if he were performing for a crowd rather than chatting with three young children. The gesture proved quite difficult for the old man, and his bones groaned from the effort.

"This was what was in those big crates?" asked Nancy.

"Some of them, yes," answered Dr. Fell. He reached up with a jerking motion and carefully adjusted his top hat, watching dozens of children play to their hearts' content on his amazing gift. After a long sigh, he glanced down at Gail, Nancy, and Jerry as if startled to see them standing there.

"Well now!" he exclaimed. "Shouldn't you three be running amok within and throughout my magnanimous neighborhood donation?"

They just looked at him. He cleared his throat.

"What I mean to say is . . . don't you want to go play?"

They returned their attention to all the children scrambling wildly over the wooden structure. For some reason, whatever spell had been cast over the rest of the children hadn't quite taken hold of them just yet.

"I . . . I have homework," said Gail, who did have homework and felt an obligation to do it.

"Yeah. Me too," said Nancy, who also had homework but felt no obligation to do it.

"I don't," said Jerry, who always finished his homework on the bus ride home from school.

"How fortuitous," said Dr. Fell, smiling. "Revelry calls."

As Gail and Nancy watched, slightly concerned, Jerry took first one step toward the playground, then another. Then a third. Then he stopped.

"It does look like fun," he said.

"Your fellow whippersnappers certainly find it so," cooed Dr. Fell.

Jerry took another step toward the playhouse, then turned to look at his sister. Gail gave him the slightest of head shakes, her eyes open and begging.

It was enough to tip the scales.

"I forgot," said Jerry. "There's a . . . a TV show . . . that I want to watch."

"A television program?" asked Dr. Fell through his smile. "On a beautiful spring afternoon such as this?"

"Yeah. Our folks recorded it for me last night. It's about nature. I've really been looking forward to seeing it. All day."

The expression on Dr. Fell's face did not change. Outwardly, he maintained an air of relaxed pleasantness. Nevertheless, the hairs on the arms of the three children stood on end under his welcoming, hyena-like smile.

"Another day, perhaps," said the very old man.

"Definitely," agreed Jerry, backing away. "Another day."

They turned and walked home as calmly as they could, well aware of Dr. Fell's gaze drilling into their spines as they retreated from his yard.

Left in their wake were countless neighborhood children screaming with delight as they took full advantage of the unexpected wonderland that had popped up in the blink of an eye.

Their joyful cries echoed for miles in all directions.

Chapter 4

The Need for Dr. Fell

THE PLAYGROUND OF DR. FELL was covered with a thin layer of children at all times.

They swarmed over it in the morning before school. They answered its siren call in the afternoon when school was over. Some of the braver children raced back on their bikes during lunch to enjoy just five minutes on the wondrous structure before hurrying back to school in time for the end-of-lunch bell. On Wednesday, Zachary Fallowmold and Johnny Doomburg skipped school entirely to scramble through its fantastic passageways.

They were caught by Johnny's mother, PTA Co-President Martha Doomburg, and grounded for a week.

But it was worth it.

Nearly everyone living on Hardscrabble Street, Vexington Avenue, Von Burden Lane, and Turnabout Road (Old Lady Witherton could not be bothered) agreed that they had never seen the neighborhood's children so enthralled and obsessed with the same thing at the same time. Certainly there had been the week when Hannah Festerworth had received a Puking Pony doll for her birthday and every girl in the area had wanted to play with it (forcing Janice Festerworth to replace her entire living room carpet), but none of the boys had cared. And of course there was the time Gore Oozewuld had been given a set of Flaming Nunchucks for Bleeding Martyr's Day and every boy in the area had wanted to try them (forcing Olga Oozewuld to throw out her overly flammable dining room table), but none of the girls had cared.

But boy and girl, toddler and teen, right-handed and left-handed, all craved the playground of Dr. Fell.

Not a free moment went by that screams of glee did not sound from within its depths.

So it was only a matter of time before they were replaced by screams of pain.

It was little Ethel Pusster, younger sister of Ethan Pusster, who became the playground's first victim. The spunky six-year-old was swinging from bar to bar, leaping from platform to platform, and shimmying from pole to pole when she tripped over a slightly warped plank none of the children had noticed. She fell to the ground, landing poorly on the seemingly soft grass, and let out a wail of pain.

Instantly, the gnarled and bent form of Dr. Fell was at her side, appearing as if by magic.

"There, there, my sweet groundling," he cooed. "Tears need not fall from such a pretty face. Let us have a look at your reprehensible boo-boo, shall we?"

Ethel blinked up into Dr. Fell's wide, milky eyes and tried to hold back her tears of pain like a big girl. "I—I—hurt—my—kneeeeee—" she said in halting, choke-filled gasps.

The other children gravitated toward Ethel and Dr. Fell, unable to resist the spectacle of an injured playmate.

"So I see, little one. So I see," said Dr. Fell, gently examining the body part in question. "Does it hurt when I do this?"

He touched his thumb to the side of her knee. Ethel shook her head.

"Does it hurt when I do this?"

He touched his thumb to the inside of her knee. Ethel shook her head.

"Does it hurt when I do this?"

He slowly reached up and touched his thumb to his own nose. Ethel giggled.

"That's a very good sign. A very good sign indeed."

As the giggle lingered in the child's smile, he leaned forward with an audible groan and inspected her knee. A small streak of blood trickled amid the pink flesh—pinker than normal, as a good layer had been scoured off when the child had fallen onto the grass. He hummed softly to himself as he examined the minor wound, then stood up, pausing momentarily as one or more of his elderly bones protested the movement with a creak.

"Is it bad?" asked Ethel.

The other children leaned in to hear his answer.

"Well now," he said, "I am of the learned opinion that you have suffered what we in the medical profession call a skinned knee. Why don't you come inside, and I'll fix you right as rain."

"Inside?" asked Ethel.

No one had been inside the home of Dr. Fell since his unannounced arrival the week before.

"I think maybe I should get my mom," said Ethan Pusster with a nervous glance at his sister.

"Indeed," agreed Dr. Fell. "That is an excellent idea, young man. Why don't you run home and fetch the fine Mrs. Pusster whilst I attend to your sister's injury. Please come right on in when you return."

A hush fell over the children. Something seemed off, but nobody could quite put a finger on it. Some looked at Ethan. Some looked at Ethel. Some looked at Dr. Fell. Randy Macabrador looked longingly at the playhouse, eager to climb back up and continue playing.

"Come, my sweet young urchin," charmed Dr. Fell, extending a hand down to Ethel Pusster. "I have a bottle of antiseptic ointment and a bandage with your name on them."

Ethan ran home to fetch his mother while the other kids slowly dispersed, though with many a curious glance over their shoulders. Dr. Fell gently brought Ethel Pusster to her feet, allowing her to lean on his frail and fragile body. Arm in arm, they limped (she due to her skinned knee and he due to his advanced age) across the porch to his front door. The aged healer turned the doorknob, opened his door, and gestured for the little girl to hobble inside.

She was instantly swallowed up by the darkness within.

Ethan Pusster returned to the home of Dr. Fell with a very flustered and worried mother. Edna Pusster had dropped everything and come at once—leaving an apple crisp to burn in the oven in the process. Though only four houses away, the journey had seemed eternal, and she had repeatedly berated her son for allowing his six-year-old sister to enter the strange man's home all alone.

"We simply don't know what sort of man Dr. Fell is!" she huffed between strides. "He could be dangerous! He could be a maniac!"

"Yes, Mom," said Ethan, knowing better than to say anything else in response.

They hurried up the driveway and Edna leaped up the front steps two at a time—her nimbleness a legacy from her days as a high school track star.

"How dare the man abduct a small, helpless girl into his home like this!"

"Yes, Mom."

"I'm going to give him a piece of my mind, so help me God!"

"Yes, Mom."

She raised her fist and pounded on the door.

"He said to go right in, Mom," said Ethan.

She went right in.

When she exited the home some time later with her children, Edna was all smiles.

Little Ethel Pusster, fresh bandage on her knee, grinned up at her mother. "What a nice man is Dr. Fell," she said, and then she scampered off to continue playing on the play structure. She was quickly followed by her big brother. A much-relieved Edna Pusster beamed as her children played.

Last to step into the sunlight was a very satisfied-looking Dr. Fell, absently stroking the chain of his gold pocket watch.

"I'm so sorry for my behavior a moment ago, Dr. Fell," said Mrs. Pusster.

"Not at all, my dear woman. Not at all," said Dr. Fell with a wheeze. "Your baby was in harm's way. It is perfectly natural for a mother to be emotional in such situations."

Edna Pusster blushed. "You may be right, Dr. Fell, but I had no right to call you a raving, deranged madman in your own home."

"Please, good Mrs. Pusster. Consider the matter forgotten."

"Thank you so much for taking care of my little Ethel. She can be a bit clumsy at times. Always bumping into things or tripping over her own feet."

"A child who makes it through childhood without skinning a few knees is a child who has not lived," said Dr. Fell. "It was a minor matter, no more. She is already as good as new."

"I had no idea you were an actual doctor, Dr. Fell. It is such a boon to have you in our neighborhood."

"You are too kind, indeed, Mrs. Pusster. Too kind, indeed."

And with that, Edna Pusster went home and baked a new apple crisp from scratch.

She had little Ethel deliver it to Dr. Fell personally.

Chapter 5

The Services of Dr. Fell

ALTHOUGH THE NUMBER OF people living on Hardscrabble Street, Vexington Avenue, Von Burden Lane, and Turnabout Road remained unchanged, the number of children playing on the playground of Dr. Fell continued to increase. Soon, children from the neighboring neighborhoods of Passable Road, Pleasant Lane, Mildwood Avenue, and Simple Street joined in the fun. They were soon followed by the younger residents of such locations as Warthog Hill, Wombat Wash, and Wildebeest Manor. Even the children from the far-off gated communities of Tinsel Terrace and Superior Acres found themselves drawn to this mecca of childhood play.

It was as if a black hole had opened up at the end of

Hardscrabble Street and every child attending McKinley Grant Fillmore Elementary School was slowly but surely being sucked in by its gravity.

Naturally, with so many energetic children exploring the wonderland's nooks and crannies, the number of minor injuries experienced rose exponentially. However, the good Dr. Fell was always on hand to lead the tearful patient inside his home and administer whatever medical remedy was required. Without fail, the child would emerge from the house none the worse for wear and eager to rejoin his or her fellow rapscallions on the playground, hesitating only long enough to mutter, "What a nice man is Dr. Fell."

Sometimes they muttered this to an empty porch.

Nearly all the adults of Hardscrabble Street, Vexington Avenue, Von Burden Lane, and Turnabout Road (Old Lady Witherton could not be bothered) became accustomed to the medical capabilities of Dr. Fell. In fact, PTA Co-President Candice Gloomfellow approached Dr. Fell less than a week after poor little Ethel Pusster's scrape and asked if he would perform her son Christian's yearly physical.

"Normally I wouldn't bother you, as I'm sure you are retired and well deserving of your rest," she said on a bright, sunny afternoon as they stood on Dr. Fell's porch and watched the horde of children scuttle and dither about the playground. "It's just that Christian's regular physician is all the way out in Plainsboro, and it seems a waste to drive all that way when a perfectly wonderful doctor is right down the street."

The corners of Dr. Fell's mouth rose just the slightest

bit, though one could see his entire face tiring from the effort. He slowly lowered a blue glass from which he'd been sipping a yellow liquid through a red straw to reply.

"My dearest Madam Gloomfellow," he said, "I am without words to express the rapture I feel within my thankfully still-beating heart at your faith in me. That you would entrust the well-being of your offspring to my aged, knobby hands fills me with exultation."

PTA Co-President Candice Gloomfellow continued smiling, but her slightly furrowed brow led Dr. Fell to add, "What I mean to say is . . . I'd be delighted."

At this, PTA Co-President Candice Gloomfellow exhaled with relief. "Oh, thank you! Thank you, Dr. Fell!" she cried vigorously. "Do you take insurance?"

It turned out that Dr. Fell did indeed accept all forms of health insurance, though many marveled that his prices were so low, they needn't bother with insurance at all. Thus it was that Dr. Fell's calendar was soon full as appointment after appointment was made for every child on Hardscrabble Street, Vexington Avenue, Von Burden Lane, and Turnabout Road, as well as a great many other places.

For the most part, the children were thrilled to learn they had an impending appointment with Dr. Fell.

For the most part.

"I had a physical two months ago!" complained Gail Bloom.

"Yes, dear, but you're growing so quickly these days," replied her mother, Stephanie Bloom. "We just want to make sure everything's where it should be."

"If your pituitary gland isn't making enough growth hormone, it could stunt your growth," agreed Jerry.

Gail tossed her little brother a withering glare before returning her attention to her parents. "I'm fine! I don't need to see Dr. Fell!"

"You're not qualified to diagnose yourself, Gail Bird. You're not a trained physician," noted her father, Jonathan Bloom, using the pet name he'd had for her since she was a baby and which she'd hated for almost as long. "That's why we want you to see Dr. Fell."

Despite the utter ridiculousness of her parents' argument, Gail choked down her defiance. She knew nothing she said would change their minds. Once her mother and father came to a decision, it might as well be written in quick-drying cement.

"But tomorrow?" she asked plaintively, grasping at one final straw. "In the middle of the school day?"

"We're lucky he had an opening," remarked Stephanie Bloom.

"You'll stay home from school tomorrow," decided Jonathan Bloom. "To make sure you're not late for your appointment."

The Bloom parents nodded at each other in agreement, convinced that keeping a child home from school for an unnecessary medical exam was an example of good parenting.

Gail dropped her head and closed her eyes in defeat.

"Chin up, Gail Bird. There's probably nothing wrong with you," said Jonathan Bloom, incorrectly assessing the reason for his daughter's anxiety about her forthcoming medical appointment. "And if there is anything wrong, why you'll already be in Dr. Fell's office! He'll fix you up right as rain!"

"What a nice man is Dr. Fell," agreed Stephanie Bloom.

"Now, there's at least fifteen minutes before your bedtime," said a grinning Jonathan Bloom. "Why don't the two of you go play on Dr. Fell's playground?"

Brother and sister looked first at their parents, then at each other, then out the window at the sliver of moon that utterly failed to provide even a suggestion of light up and down the darkened sidewalks of Hardscrabble Street.

"You want us to go play outside now?" asked Jerry. "In the dark?"

"Your eyes will adjust," reasoned Stephanie Bloom.

"Go on," agreed Jonathan Bloom. "Go play."

Gail and Jerry each had the uncomfortable feeling that their father's words weren't so much a suggestion as a command.

"Do you want to walk over to that playground?" asked Jerry as he and his sister stood outside on their porch, each silently noting just how very dark it truly was outside.

Gail carefully peered through the blackness down the length of Hardscrabble Street before shaking her head.

Jerry let out a medium-sized sigh of relief. "Me neither," he said.

"It just doesn't make any sense," said Gail.

"I know," responded Jerry. "We can't even see a foot in front of our faces—how are we supposed to play on that thing without getting hurt?"

"It's not just that. Why are Mom and Dad so determined to make me see Dr. Fell all of a sudden?"

"Maybe they're suffering from heavy metal poisoning. It can confuse the nervous system and make you mentally unstable."

Gail shot her brother a raised eyebrow in response to this factual explanation.

"Well, it can," mumbled Jerry in defense.

"They're acting strange," declared Gail.

"It's like they're not themselves," agreed Jerry.

"Like they're under a spell."

"These days everyone on Hardscrabble Street, Vexington Avenue, Von Burden Lane, and Turnabout Road seems to be under a spell," lamented Jerry. "Except Old Lady Witherton, who really can't be bothered."

"Right. They're all obsessed with Dr. Fell," decided Gail. "What is it about him that has everybody acting so weird?"

"Maybe he's a witch?" suggested Jerry. "Well, not a witch, since witches are all women. But he's a . . . what's the male equivalent of a witch?"

"A wizard?"

"That doesn't sound nasty enough."

"An evil wizard."

"That's better."

They paused their conversation to allow time for proper reflection upon the possibility that Dr. Fell was an evil wizard. It made the tiniest bit of sense and explained some of the odd things that had happened since his arrival.

Except . . .

"Why aren't we under his spell?" asked a very astute Jerry.

Gail just shrugged.

A cloud drifted across the meager hint of moon, erasing the last source of light in the night sky.

"So what are you going to do about your appointment tomorrow?" asked Jerry finally.

"Go, I guess. I don't really have a good reason not to."

"You could pretend to be sick," suggested Jerry.

Gail tossed him yet another raised eyebrow.

"Oh, right. You're going to the doctor," finished Jerry.

A sudden crack split the night, as if someone or something prowling the darkness had accidentally stepped on a brittle twig. Both brother and sister flinched, then looked around.

"What was that?" asked Gail.

"It could be a coyote," answered Jerry unconvincingly. "Or maybe a raccoon."

"That was much bigger than a raccoon."

Without their noticing, Gail and Jerry's hands found each other as the siblings strained their eyes to peer into the black. Finally, Gail broke the silence. "We must have been out here long enough. Come on, let's go back inside."

"Yeah," agreed Jerry. "I think that's a good idea."

Just then, the cloud covering the thin crescent moon slid away, allowing the natural world around them to be bathed in a soft blue glow, which momentarily chased away the pitch-black darkness.

Jerry stared in shock.

Gail stared in confusion.

"I don't remember walking here," whispered Jerry.

"I don't remember walking anywhere," whispered Gail.

Less than a foot away from them stood the playground of Dr. Fell.

They ran home as quickly as possible.

Chapter 6

Gail's Appointment with Dr. Fell

THE NEXT MORNING, GAIL joined her brother at the bus stop. She told her mother she just wanted to make sure the easily distracted eight-year-old actually got on the bus, but the truth was, she wanted to tell Nancy about her appointment with Dr. Fell later in the day.

"Are you scared?" asked her best friend.

"It's just a physical," answered Gail automatically, though without much conviction.

"I know," said Nancy. "But still . . . you know . . ."

"Yeah," agreed Gail. "I know."

Nothing more needed to be said. Gail promised Nancy (and the overly nosey Jerry) that she'd give a full report on her appointment when she returned to school later that day, then waved good-bye as the school bus coughed up a mechanical lungful of toxic exhaust with a grinding wheeze and puttered away down Hardscrabble Street. Nancy and Jerry, sitting in the back of the bus, waved at Gail through the windows of the rear emergency door until the dingy yellow vehicle turned the corner and drove out of sight.

Later that morning, Stephanie Bloom ducked her head into her daughter's room. "Are you ready to see Dr. Fell?" she asked.

Gail sighed and set aside the book she'd been reading. Though truth be told, she hadn't so much been reading as staring blankly at it for the past hour without turning a page. "I guess," she answered.

"You don't sound excited, sweetie," noticed her mother.

"Why should I be excited to get a physical?"

"It's not just any physical, sweetie. It's a physical from Dr. Fell."

Stephanie Bloom beamed proudly at Gail, as if her daughter had worked hard and overcome countless obstacles to earn the amazing prize of a yearly physical. For her part, Gail moaned, groaned, and rolled her eyes in response.

Inwardly.

Outwardly she nodded her head and got to her feet like a good girl.

"Let me just get my shoes on," she said.

"Great idea, sweetie. I'll get mine on and we can wait by the door until it's time for your appointment."

"What do you mean? When's the appointment?"

"Eleven o'clock. Sharp."

Gail glanced at her clock, then, deciding a glance wasn't enough, turned her entire head to get a good look and make sure she'd read the clock correctly.

"Mom, it's barely nine-thirty."

"We don't want to be late," chimed Stephanie Bloom.

"Dr. Fell lives, like, four houses down from us!"

"Don't worry, I'll make sure we have plenty of time for the trip. Now grab your shoes and meet me by the front door."

With that, her mother's head ducked back out of the room, leaving Gail the privacy she needed to safely moan, groan, and roll her eyes. For real this time.

After almost a solid hour of sitting by the front door in two chairs her mother had dragged over from the living room, it was time to go. While her mother quickly touched up her makeup and smoothed her new red paisley dress, Gail stood and tried not to gawk at the sight of Stephanie Bloom in a dress. It wasn't that Gail had never seen her mother in a dress before—she was pretty sure her mom had worn one to at least the first half of Aunt Anita's wedding the year before; it was just that Gail found the idea of her mother wearing a dress to her daughter's physical incredibly disturbing.

Once Stephanie Bloom was satisfied she looked her best and that Gail looked as good as she was ever going to look, mother ushered daughter out the door.

It was ten-thirty in the morning.

The walk down Hardscrabble Street was excruciatingly slow. Gail's mother moved in spurts and stops, torn between the fear of arriving late and the embarrassment of arriving early. In the end, even stretching the five-minute walk out to twelve minutes, the Bloom women arrived on the porch of Dr. Fell with well over fifteen minutes to spare.

As her mother straightened her hair and knocked on the door, Gail's eyes found themselves taking in the majestic playground beckoning a few yards away. Even now, in the middle of a school day, easily a dozen children clambered all over it, their giggles of merriment echoing off the structure and bouncing around in her ear.

What was it about that playground that had everybody so obsessed? It was a nice playground, to be sure, and there were a lot of really cool-looking platforms and gizmos and whatnots. And yes, she admitted to herself, it looked like there were some great places from which to jump to the ground. And there supposedly was an awesome rope swing in there somewhere, according to Hannah Festerworth. And Gail had to admit she was curious to explore the hollowed-out tomb Gabby Plaugestein had mentioned in passing the other day. And hadn't somebody talked about a zero-G section? That sounded totally—

"Ah, Madam Bloom," croaked Dr. Fell in a froglike whisper. "I am invigorated to find your ever-pleasing beauty upon the threshold of my domicile. I yearn to verify the physical well-being of your sprightly little cherub."

Gail spun her attention back to the door, annoyed at herself for thinking . . . for thinking . . . What had she just been thinking?

"Oh!" responded a suddenly flustered Stephanie Bloom. "Oh! Well! I . . . that is . . . I . . ."

Dr. Fell's mouth struggled to transform into a smile beneath his purple top hat. "What I mean to say is . . . good morning."

"Yes," agreed Stephanie Bloom. "Yes, it is a very good morning."

The goodness of the morning agreed upon, Dr. Fell took a sip of yellow liquid from an orange glass through a chartreuse-colored straw and turned his rickety neck to look down at his patient—though for some reason, Gail felt it wasn't quite as rickety as it had been the other day. "Are you ready for your physical, my dear urchin?"

He pulled his door wide, inviting the Blooms to enter. Mother stepped aside to make room for daughter, but daughter hesitated. Gail did not want to go inside the home of Dr. Fell. Her feet did not want to step over the threshold, her legs did not want to walk into the beckoning darkness, and her arms did not want to let go of the porch railing she hadn't even known she was clutching. Every muscle in her body twitched with the desire to turn and run from the kindly old man dressed all in black. It was as if Dr. Fell were the negative electrical charge to Gail's positive one, pushing her away with invisible force.

"Sweetie?" asked her mother.

A stronger-willed child might have fled. A stronger-willed child might have listened to the drumbeat of intuition and refused point-blank to enter the ominous home of the equally ominous Dr. Fell.

Unfortunately for Gail, she was not particularly strong willed.

"Yes, Mother," she said, silently telling her intuition to stuff it.

Defeated, she trudged forth.

Gail had no idea what she'd find upon entering the living room of Dr. Fell. She certainly knew the layout of the room from her time cavorting through the house before Dr. Fell had moved in, but she had no idea how he might have furnished and decorated it. A white, sterile examination room? A dusty, junk-filled room that smelled like old people? A torture chamber? The possibilities were so vast, she didn't think anything could surprise her.

She was wrong.

"Do you have cats, Dr. Fell?" asked her mother.

"I do not," replied Dr. Fell with effort. "I have never been one to fraternize with family Felidae. I find them eternally boorish and judgmental."

Once again, Stephanie Bloom seemed utterly lost by the words of Dr. Fell. However, before she could ask for clarification, her daughter (who had at least figured out that Dr. Fell did not like cats) interrupted.

"If you don't like them, then why . . . ?" She gestured to the walls of the living room.

"Ah, yes, my patients find them soothing," explained Dr. Fell.

Soothing was not a word Gail would have used. Disturbing, perhaps. Obsessive, certainly. Creepy, quite possibly.

The walls of the living room were covered with

photographs of kittens. There were kittens sitting on chairs, kittens lying on beds, kittens playing with balls, kittens chasing mice, kittens peeking out from under pillows, kittens drinking milk, kittens wrestling with other kittens, kittens jumping out of windows, kittens driving cars, kittens dressed as mailmen, kittens dueling with light sabers, and—in a picture hanging above the fireplace—a kitten made up to look like a clown.

Definitely creepy.

In addition to the abundance of kittens, the room boasted an additional peculiarity—the color purple. The couch was purple, the chairs were purple, the curtains were purple, the desk was purple. The coffee table was not purple but so keenly shined that it acted as a mirror, reflecting the vomit of purple surrounding it.

Beyond creepy.

A hacking cough pulled both Gail's and Stephanie's attention away from the startling decor and back to Dr. Fell, who wiped the spittle from his lips with a lavender handkerchief monogrammed with a trio of very ornate letter *F*s.

"Now then, my fine young specimen," said Dr. Fell, attempting to stuff the handkerchief into a jacket pocket with one trembling hand while placing his glass on a side table with the other. "Shall we commence with your rudimentary physical examination?"

Gail's face flushed with sudden panic. "Right here?" she asked.

Dr. Fell tried unsuccessfully to laugh at Gail's outburst, turning what had been intended as a display of good-natured amusement into a slightly diabolical cackle. "Heavens, no! I do not well believe the state board of medicine would look fondly upon my performing even the smallest of medical procedures within such a stuffy, dingy, unclean environment," he said. "I have . . . a room."

Dr. Fell pointed, and Gail followed the crooked line of his finger toward a dark, stout oak door (which Gail did not recall being there when the house had been vacant) bearing a photograph of two kittens performing *The Nutcracker.*

"Wonderful!" Gail's mother clapped. "I must say, Dr. Fell, I'm so excited to see you in action! You've been such a boon to the neighborhood."

"I do thank you for your praise, Madam Bloom," he responded. "However, my responsibility as an upstanding member of the medical profession demands that I allow your child the luxury of privacy during her examination, should she wish."

"Do I really have to have a full physical?" asked Gail one last time. "I feel fine. Honest."

"I am afraid I must put my foot down," said Dr. Fell, who then spent a good minute in an attempt to demonstrate putting his foot down, an activity that involved a fair amount of wobbling before he leaned on one of his purple chairs to steady himself. "A young one's well-being is best served through preventative care. I would be remiss to allow you to neglect your health. Fret not—we will not be long."

He reached out as if to pat her on the head, but the

shriveled muscles of his arm protested the effort and he eventually stopped trying.

Gail came very close to frowning in front of her mother. Out of ideas, she visibly deflated, ready to accept her fate, though not without the simplest of precautions. "Mom can come," she said quickly.

"Indeed," agreed Dr. Fell. "For her sake as well as yours, as I've yet to accumulate a proper collection of magazines. I'm afraid the only periodical I could offer you, Mrs. Bloom, is the latest edition of *Blimp Enthusiast*."

"*Blimp Enthusiast*! One of my favorites!" cheered Stephanie Bloom, spying the lone magazine sitting on one end of the couch.

"Is it really? I am so pleased." Dr. Fell did not look so much pleased as amused. "What a coincidence. I, too, find comfort and pleasure in reading about zeppelins. That is my personal copy, but you are welcome to examine its pages whilst I examine your daughter, if you like."

Gail furrowed her brow with apprehension. Of all the magazines in the world, what were the odds that Dr. Fell would own a copy of her mother's favorite?

Again. Creepy.

"If we're all set then," said Dr. Fell with just a hint of eagerness, "let us commence."

Gail looked at the large door with the dancing kitties, then back at her mother—already on the couch and devouring the latest issue of *Blimp Enthusiast*. This was a bad idea. Something was wrong. Something important.

"Do I have to?" she asked her mother, grasping at a final straw.

"Yes, sweetie," answered her mother without looking up from the engrossing pages of her magazine. "You have to."

And for Gail Bloom, that sealed the deal. Resigned, she walked over to the heavy, ominous door, turned the handle, and stepped inside.

Chapter 7

The Miracle of Dr. Fell

"AND THEN WHAT?" ASKED Nancy Pinkblossom as she and Jerry sat across from Gail at lunch and listened to her story.

"And then I had my examination," said Gail.

"Yeah, but what happened?" pressed Nancy.

"What, you've never had a routine physical?"

"Of course I have, but I haven't had one done by Dr. Fell."

"Did he check your blood pressure? Look down your throat? Listen to your heart with a stethoscope?" asked Jerry.

"Yes," replied Gail.

"What was the room like?" asked Nancy.

"It was a room," answered Gail.

"But what kind of room?" begged Jerry. "Sparkling white like a doctor's office? Purple like his living room? A big room? A little room?"

"It was a room."

Feeling the matter settled, Gail took a bite of her ham-and-cheese sandwich.

Nancy and Jerry shared a look, and for one of the first times in their squabbling lives it was a look of neither venom nor disdain.

"Oh, I see," said Nancy, who did not see. "We're just really curious about the guy, that's all."

Somebody nodded. Somebody else nodded. The subject was dropped and more food was eaten in silence.

So awkwardly quiet was the remainder of the three children's lunch that Nancy and Jerry were able to hear Gail quietly mumble to herself, "What a nice man is Dr. Fell."

"I'm worried about your sister," whispered Nancy when she managed to catch Jerry alone after school as they waited to board the school bus. "She just acted so weird at lunch when we asked her about her appointment with Dr. Fell, and then she seemed totally not there during class this afternoon. I tried to get her attention a couple of times, but she just smiled at me. And I'm pretty sure I caught her mouthing 'What a nice man is Dr. Fell' to herself a few times. That's just not like her. I mean, you know her pretty good, being her little brother and all. What do you think?"

Jerry's first thought was to point out that Nancy had just spoken to him for twenty-one seconds straight without calling him a name, but he chose instead to focus on their mutual concern. "She didn't eat all her lunch," Jerry pointed out. "She usually feels obligated to eat everything because Mom goes to all the trouble to pack it for her. Something's definitely wrong."

"Do you think Dr. Fell got to her?"

It was the undeniable conclusion, but before Jerry could answer, Gail joined them in line.

"Hi," she said with a dreamy look on her face.

"Hi," said Nancy and Jerry carefully in response, as if afraid to make any sudden movements around their friend and sister.

Gail smiled. Nancy and Jerry smiled—on the outside. On the inside, they nervously waited for a sign either proving or disproving that Gail had fallen under the spell of Dr. Fell.

For her part, Gail was smiling on the inside as well.

"What do you want to do when we get home?" asked Nancy, testing the waters.

"Play on the playground of Dr. Fell!" cheered Gail.

It appeared that Dr. Fell had indeed cast his spell.

So it was that for the first time since its magical appearance, the playground of Dr. Fell hosted Gail and Jerry Bloom and Nancy Pinkblossom. They joined the dozens of other children scrambling over its offerings. Gail hit the playground with abandon, leaping from platform to platform, swinging from bar to bar, and climbing up wall after wall. Like the rest of the children at play, she moved with a fluidity rarely seen in a preteen—her body contorting and bending in all the right places and at all the right times to take full advantage of the wondrous structure.

Nancy and Jerry were more deliberate in their play, with Nancy doing her best to keep up with Gail without knocking anyone else over and Jerry doing his best not to get knocked over himself, since as usual nobody seemed to notice he was even there. Each kept an eye on Gail at all times, each did their best to keep up with the frantic flow of childish glee on display, and each silently admitted that it was, indeed, a truly awesome play structure. The large number of hooligans-in-training cavorting on the playhouse made it difficult for the two sworn enemies to find moments alone to compare notes on Gail's actions and movements, so they tried their best to keep a mental list of everything they saw, with the hope that they would be able to meet up at a later point in time to discuss their findings about their friend and sister.

As luck would have it, Fate chose this particular afternoon, rather than any that had come before, to unveil the first true medical emergency to occur on the playground of Dr. Fell. This was not lucky for Bud Fetidsky, the injured child in question, but rather for Nancy Pinkblossom and Jerry Bloom, who witnessed the traumatic turn of events.

The incident began with Bud swinging head over heels on a bar while squealing with glee. He was currently saving Planet Earth from an invasion by the Mighty Meaty Insect Empire (with the help of both Randy Macabrador and Albert Rottingsly), blasting his invisible ray gun at invisible

Mighty Meaty Insects while zipping through the atmosphere in his invisible solar-powered rocket jet.

Suddenly Randy called out that a patrol of Mighty Meaty Insects had landed near the boys' interstellar space rocket. Bud knew he had to join his fellow Earth Protectors and blast some bugs, so he twirled, spun, and leaped off the bar to a nearby platform.

Except the platform wasn't where he thought it was.

So rather than landing catlike on the platform and running to Earth's aid, Bud Fetidsky slammed a knee against the edge of a wall. This caused him to slam his other knee against a bar he didn't remember, to bang his head against a platform he did remember, and to land very, very poorly on the shockingly hard ground he wouldn't soon forget.

Almost every child on the playground heard the telltale snap of bone and Bud Fetidsky's scream of agony.

Nancy and Jerry were quickly by Bud's side, seemingly more concerned about their peer than any of the other children. Not that the others didn't also gather around their fallen friend, but most of them, including Gail, seemed content with standing around waiting for somebody else to do something.

"Are you all right?" asked Nancy, though she knew it was about as dumb a question as one could possibly ask a child who was writhing on the ground howling in pain.

"Get back! Give him air!" yelled Jerry. "He may have just had the wind knocked out of—"

None of the children ever learned what Jerry thought

Bud had had the wind knocked out of. Not because they weren't really paying attention to Jerry (though they weren't) but because Bud rolled over, and everyone could see that his leg was bent in cruel and inhuman ways.

"My, my," wheezed Dr. Fell, seeming to appear out of nowhere, then kneeling by Bud's side. "You've taken quite a tumble, my dear lad."

Bud screamed as if to confirm the true extent of his tumble.

"Yes, I imagine you are in a great deal of severe pain at this particular moment, my fine young rapscallion," continued Dr. Fell. "You're going to require medical attention. Happily, I have an opening. Come, let us see to your most unfortunate injury."

Showing far more strength than any of the kids had thought possible, Dr. Fell scooped his arms under the wailing child and lifted him into the air.

"Could one or more of you fine young children inform this poor lad's mother of both his current state of physical torment and his whereabouts?"

With the children by now used to the odd way in which Dr. Fell spoke, several of them turned and ran to fetch the Fetidskys.

"There, there, young man," said Dr. Fell soothingly to his miserable charge. "We shall have you fixed up in no time."

Dr. Fell carried Bud Fetidsky into his home. Show over, most of the other children returned to their play. Nancy and Jerry, however, stood rooted to the spot.

"His leg . . . ," began Nancy.

". . . not supposed to bend that way," finished Jerry.

They remained standing at the scene of the accident for some time in an unspoken desire to watch events unfold. Soon, Mabel Fetidsky came hurrying down Hardscrabble Street, her immense bulk jiggling as she ran. She launched herself up the front steps and into the home of Dr. Fell, her face a mask of worry.

She was still in there when the coming darkness forced Nancy and Jerry and most of the other kids to finally head home.

Bud Fetidsky was not at school the next day.

"He probably won't be back for a while," reasoned Jerry aloud at lunch. Neither Nancy nor Gail was paying him any attention, however. Nancy was busy scrutinizing Gail, and Gail was busy smiling to herself. "A broken leg can take forever to heal, and Bud's leg was about as broken as you can get. He'll probably be on crutches for months. Do you think he'll let me sign his cast?"

Neither girl answered him.

Bud Fetidsky did not let Jerry sign his cast.

This was not due to any animosity Bud felt toward Jerry, but rather was due to the fact that when Bud Fetidsky returned to school a single day later, his leg was not in a cast. Instead, he wore a simple wooden splint that caused his leg to itch so badly, he removed it during fifth period. That afternoon he was once again saving the Earth from the Mighty Meaty Insect Empire with the help of both Randy Macabrador and Albert Rottingsly.

The only indication that he had literally snapped his leg in half two days earlier was a slight limp that itself was gone in one more day.

"That's ... that's impossible," said Jerry, standing with Nancy and Gail in front of the always-crowded play structure.

"Maybe it wasn't as bad a break as we thought," suggested Nancy.

"No way," refuted Jerry. "You saw it. He snapped it in half."

"I don't see what the big deal is," said Gail. "He went and saw Dr. Fell, so of course he's OK."

With that, Gail joined the other children on the playground.

Chapter 8

The Unexpected Alliance Brought On by Dr. Fell

"MOM? DAD? HAVE EITHER of you noticed anything weird with Gail lately?" Jerry stood just inside the kitchen Friday morning while his parents busied themselves with their rituals of drinking coffee and surfing the Internet on their iPads.

"Weird?" grunted Jonathan Bloom, who needed at least three cups of coffee before he could speak in multiword sentences.

"Your sister is the same sweet young darling she's always been, Jerry," answered his mother. "Why do you ask?"

Jerry dropped his gaze and kicked absently at the floor for a moment. "She just seems . . . I dunno . . . I was just . . ." He gave up. How could he tell his parents he thought Dr.

Fell had brainwashed their daughter if they were also under the odious man's spell?

"'S fine," mumbled his father as he poured his third cup of coffee.

"But . . . but . . ." Jerry's increasing sense of desperation caused him to stumble over his words. "I mean, where is she right now? It's almost time for the bus! Gail never misses the bus!"

"Your sister ate her breakfast almost an hour ago," purred Stephanie Bloom. "She got up early so she'd have time to play."

The blood drained from Jerry's face, turning it a sickly shade of pale. "Play?"

"She's outside on Dr. Fell's playground," his mother confirmed.

Nancy Pinkblossom was grumpy.

For some reason, her mother hadn't yet left for work when Nancy came out of her room, which had created an awkward period during which they each sat at the table eating breakfast feeling like they shouldn't ignore each other but not having anything to say. It wasn't that Nancy and her mother disliked each other; it was simply that ever since Mr. Pinkblossom had left a few years ago, Nancy had resented her mother for whatever she assumed her mother had done to drive him away. Mrs. Pinkblossom, for her part, had taken her daughter's resentment personally and had spent the better part of the last couple of years trying not to further upset her. The result had been an awkward truce in which the two tended not to interact all that much. So a breakfast of staring at each other across the table was a rotten start to each of their mornings.

And then there was school. Nancy was not a fan of school on the best of days, and today was not the best of days. For one thing, she had gym, and she hated gym. For another, the cafeteria was serving its infamous cardboard-cutout pizza, which was perfectly barfworthy. Also, Assistant Principal Richman was wearing a hideously ugly Jabba the Hutt tie in a lame attempt to be cool. Normally, Nancy would have turned to Gail and mocked their nerdy assistant principal to brighten her mood, but that wasn't possible—which was actually the worst part of the day.

Her friend was not acting like the Gail Bloom Nancy had known since she'd moved into the neighborhood during kindergarten. Instead, she was wobbling about as if in a dream, glassy-eyed and bubbleheaded. It was almost like someone else was wearing Gail's body—someone very boring. Nancy was not a fan of this new Gail, and she hoped the old Gail would show up soon and kick the imposter out.

Making things worse, if that were possible, was that every other child at McKinley Grant Fillmore Elementary School seemed equally out to lunch. They walked the halls with blank grins on their faces, oblivious to their surroundings and often bumping into one another. Sometimes an adult would steer a child away from an impending collision, but just as often the adult would simply stand and smile as one child bounced away from another with an audible thunk like a pimply pinball careening off an equally pimply bumper.

And then there was all the talk of Dr. Fell.

"Dr. Fell once saved the president's life," said fifth grader Aiden Grand.

"Dr. Fell always washes behind his ears," said fourth grader Shelly Plentyson.

"Dr. Fell is a friend to puppies," said third grader Jewel Sparkledink.

"What a nice man is Dr. Fell," said absolutely everybody.

Topping it off was the perfectly healthy Bud Fetidsky, who spent the day acting as town crier, heaping loud, public praise on Dr. Fell while leaping about on his perfectly healthy leg, which only a short while ago had been perfectly shattered.

Nancy wanted to scream.

"Don't scream," said Jerry Bloom, coming up behind her during lunch.

Nancy spun around, eyes narrowed. "Why do you say that?" she asked suspiciously, annoyed that she hadn't noticed him behind her.

"So you wouldn't scream," he answered. "When I came up behind you. I didn't want you to be startled and start screaming."

"Why are you sneaking up behind me?"

"I didn't want to, but you weren't turning around and I couldn't wait any longer to talk to you. Lunch'll be over soon."

The ten-year-old girl eyed her eight-year-old archnemesis warily. She noticed he carried a large cafeteria tray laden with not only the disgusting pizza but also three large chocolate chip cookies. "How did you get three cookies?" she asked. Lunch Lady Fortunato was notoriously stingy with the cookies, hovering over them possessively like a cat curling up around its own tail. She had even been known to hiss at children who asked for a second cookie.

"I took advantage of Lunch Lady Fortunato's fatal flaw," explained Jerry. "She has a phobia about mice in her kitchen. I released a spinning top just before I reached the cookies, and the noise drew her attention away long enough for me to grab extras."

Nancy was impressed.

"They're for you," said Jerry, extending his tray toward her.

Nancy was even more impressed.

"Why for me?" she asked.

"Because I think you and I are the only people at school who haven't been brainwashed by Dr. Fell," replied Jerry, "which means we may have to work together to fix all this."

Nancy dropped her guard. "You didn't have to give me cookies for that," she said, absently grabbing all three cookies off his tray. "I'm just as worried as you are."

Jerry set the cookie-free tray down on a table and leaned into Nancy conspiratorially. "I think it has something to do with Dr. Fell," he whispered.

A dozen snarky replies tap-danced through Nancy's mind in response, but she fought back the urge to be evil in the name of the greater good. "I think you're right," she said instead.

The bell rang, alerting any and all children that the time for lunch was over, the time for learning was about to begin, and they really should make their way to the proper classrooms as soon as possible.

As one, the students of McKinley Grant Fillmore Elementary School calmly stood, returned their trays to the counter, and walked blissfully out of the cafeteria.

It was spooky.

"I have an idea," said Jerry, backing away in his hurry to get to class. "Bring Gail to your house after school."

"What?" she asked, confused. "Why?"

"Just do it!" commanded the third grader as the tide of children swept him out of the room.

Nancy frowned. She didn't like taking orders from a third grader.

But she liked what had happened to her best friend even less.

"Why can't we go straight to Dr. Fell's playground?" asked Gail as Nancy led her up the street toward her house.

"We will, I promise," answered Nancy. "I just need to . . . I wanted to . . ." Usually she could pull a perfectly good lie out of thin air, but the one time she was trying to lie for a good cause, she was drawing a blank.

"Whatever it is, it can't be more important than playing on Dr. Fell's playground," Gail insisted.

Nancy mentally scrolled through her playlist of excuses.

It would have helped if she'd had the slightest idea what Jerry was planning. Unfortunately, she was as much in the dark as Gail—though admittedly Gail was not aware that she was in the dark.

"I need to change my clothes," Nancy finally blurted. "I don't want to get these pants dirty when I'm playing on Dr. Fell's playground."

It was a lame excuse, she knew, but her dazed friend seemed satisfied.

Approaching her front steps, she wondered how long she would need to keep Gail inside. Jerry hadn't been on the bus, so she half assumed the plan—whatever it was—was dead on arrival. But not knowing what else to do, she'd dragged her friend over, hoping against hope.

"Why don't I wait for you over at Dr. Fell's playground?" suggested Gail once they reached Nancy's front porch. The telltale siren songs of glee had begun to filter down the street as children, freed from the confines of the school bus, reached the joyful nirvana of the playground.

"No!" yelped Nancy, slightly more loudly than necessary. "No. I need your advice. On what to wear."

Nancy turned away, rolling her eyes at her own ridiculousness, and grabbed the handle of the front door with one hand while digging out the key she wore on a chain around her neck with the other.

Except the door was open.

"Whoa!" Nancy stumbled gracelessly into her house, surprised to find it unlocked.

"Is your mom home?" asked Gail, following her inside.

Instead of answering, Nancy crept into the living room, her nerves on full alert. There had been no car in the driveway, so her mother was not home. Also, the curtains had been pulled shut, blocking any and all sunlight and giving the room an undeniably ominous feel.

Something was wrong.

"On second thought, maybe we should just go to the playground," muttered Nancy, eyes searching the dark room for answers. "How does that sound?"

She was answered by a loud bang as the front door was slammed shut.

Standing behind them was Jerry Bloom, his hands behind his back and a serious look on his face.

"Not good," he said.

"Jerry!" exclaimed a startled Nancy, both surprised to find him in her house and annoyed at his having snuck up on her again. "What are you doing? How'd you get in here?"

"Do you want to play on Dr. Fell's playground too?" Gail asked innocently.

"No, Gail, I do not," said Jerry, stepping forward and holding out the rope he'd been hiding behind his back. "I have something else in mind."

"Oh?" asked Gail, still surprisingly innocent.

The eight-year-old boy raised an eyebrow, looking about as menacing as an eight-year-old can look. "We're going to have an exorcism."

Chapter 9

The Exorcism of Dr. Fell

NANCY BURST OUT LAUGHING. "An exorcism?" she asked. "Really, Dorknose?"

Jerry visibly deflated in response to Nancy's reaction, losing all traces of menace in the process. "Ah, come on! We're supposed to be partners."

"Not if you're going to be a total goober."

"I'm not a total goober!"

"I dunno. That idea sounds really gooberish."

"When are we going to Dr. Fell's playground?" interrupted Gail.

Jerry and Nancy looked from each other to their friend and sister. Nancy sighed.

"All right," she said. "What do we do?"

What they did was take Gail down into Nancy's unfinished basement, tie the surprisingly willing subject to an old metal folding chair, and stand around wondering how one conducts an exorcism.

"Aren't we supposed to sprinkle her with holy water?" asked Nancy carefully.

"That's for demons," answered Jerry equally carefully. "Is Dr. Fell a demon?"

That neither of them could truly answer this question gave them both a severe case of the willies. To be safe, Nancy filled a glass with water, waved the family Bible over it a few times, and poured it on top of Gail's head.

"What else?" she asked.

Though not an expert on exorcisms, Jerry had come prepared. He and Nancy proceeded to sprinkle salt ("Holy salt," said Jerry) on Gail's head, light candles ("Holy candles," said Jerry) and waft the smoke into Gail's face, flick specks of vegetable oil ("Holy oil," said Jerry) onto Gail's shirt, and drape a necklace of plastic craft beads ("Holy rosary beads," said Jerry) around Gail's neck.

For her part, Gail took everything in stride, not so much complaining as continually asking when this was going to be over so they could all go and play on Dr. Fell's playground.

"It's not working," remarked Nancy.

"Yeah, I know," admitted Jerry. "Maybe we should chant. There's usually a lot of chanting involved."

"What should we chant?"

This was a stumper, and the two went back and forth for

a time with ideas until settling on what they hoped was the perfect mantra.

"Dr. Fell is *not* a nice man!" they said in unison. "Dr. Fell is *not* a nice man!"

"What a horrible thing to say!" exclaimed a shocked Gail. "He's the nicest, most wonderful, most loving, most giving, most wonderful, most kind, most incredible, most wonderful man on the face of the Earth!"

Jerry and Nancy jerked back, as if Gail were a wasp and her outburst her sting. "Now, I've been very patient while you two tied me up and played your little game," she said. "I let you dump water on me, rub salt in my hair, and ruin my blouse with that oil, but the day is slipping away and we still haven't gone to Dr. Fell's playground!"

It was the straw that broke the camel's back. Or it would have been had Nancy been a camel. "Will you stop talking about that stupid playground!" she roared.

Jerry could only gasp in astonishment at the strength of Nancy's rage (relieved it was not directed at him). She jumped onto her friend's lap, sending them both toppling over—Gail backward and Nancy frontward—as the chair tipped and fell to the ground.

"Hey!" complained Gail as best she could from her now-horizontal position.

"Dr. Fell is evil!" screamed Nancy, grabbing her friend's ears to punctuate her point. "Do you hear me? Evil! Evil! Evil!"

"Nancy! Stop!"

Jerry's outburst speared its way through Nancy's fog of war, and she blinked her eyes to find herself clutching Gail's head between her sweaty hands, as if to smash it repeatedly on the ground. Of course she did no such thing, but the mere fact that she found herself astride her best friend in such a manner filled her with shame. A sob bubbled from her lips, quickly followed by a second. Then a third.

"I'm sorry," she choked out while climbing off her friend. "I'm so sorry, Gail. I just . . . I just don't want to lose you. I don't know what to do."

"I'd like to be untied now," said Gail in a surprisingly near-cheery tone.

"Of course," answered Nancy. "Right. Hold on."

"Wait!" yelled Jerry, as inspiration struck him with the savage jolt of a lightning bolt.

"What?" asked Nancy and Gail together.

"Do you still think Dr. Fell is a nice man?" he asked.

"Of course!" answered Gail. "What a nice man is Dr. Fell."

Jerry snapped his fingers. It was not a very strong snap, as Jerry did not have very strong fingers, but he was unconcerned. "Dr. Fell has everyone thinking upside down," he said, this time to Nancy.

"Yes?" said Nancy, more to urge him to continue his line of thought than due to any agreement with his rather silly hypothesis.

"So let's turn her right side up."

He smiled. Gail smiled. Nancy stared.

"Huh?" she asked.

In answer, Jerry approached the chair to which poor Gail, now lying on her back, was still bound. "Right side up," he repeated, grabbing two of the chair legs. Wordlessly, Nancy grabbed the other two, and together they lifted the chair up by its legs, with Gail, still tied to it, hanging upside down.

"I'm not sure this is a good idea," observed Gail.

But Jerry was not to be deterred. With Nancy's help, he began shaking the chair up and down as if he expected loose change to pour out of Gail's pockets. Gail screamed. Nancy screamed. Jerry screamed. Children at the end of Hardscrabble Street screamed—though their screams were ones of joy brought on by their frolic upon the play structure rather than ones of horror brought on by the torment of a young girl at the hands of the two individuals she trusted most in the entire world.

"Get out, Dr. Fell! Out!" yelled Jerry. "Get out of my sister's head!"

"Get out, Dr. Fell! Out!" yelled Nancy. "Get out of my best friend's head!"

"Stop shaking me upside down, you idiots!" yelled Gail. "This is not fun!"

Something had to give. Not surprisingly, it was the knots holding Gail to the chair. With a crash, she tumbled to the floor in a heap, the sudden lack of her weight on the chair causing Jerry and Nancy to fly backward in midshake. They, too, tumbled to the ground in heaps.

All was silence.

After a moment, the three children stirred, carefully poking their heads up like wary puppies that had just gone on the dining room rug and expected to be scolded.

"Is everybody OK?" asked Jerry. "Does anyone have a concussion?"

"I'm good," answered Nancy. "Gail?"

Gail groaned and rubbed her head where a slight bump was beginning to form. "No, I'm not OK," she grumbled. "You guys could have killed me! What were you trying to do?"

"We're trying to save you from Dr. Fell!" screamed Nancy in a sudden burst. "He's got his claws into you and turned you into one of the pod people!"

"Don't be stupid! I told you, I won't let him do anything to me. I'll go to my appointment and case the joint, then report back to—"

Gail stopped.

Nancy and Jerry also stopped, though in truth they had little to stop as they were currently staring at Gail in confusion. Which they did not stop doing. But they stopped everything else.

Somewhere outside, a dog barked.

"Wait a minute," said a suddenly uneasy Gail. "Why are we in your basement?"

Too stunned to respond, Nancy and Jerry held their breath, waiting for the other shoe to drop.

"What time is it?" continued Gail. "Why aren't you guys at school? What's going on?"

What was going on was that Gail was back.

The exorcism had worked.

Chapter 10

A Chance Encounter with Dr. Fell

IT QUICKLY BECAME APPARENT that Gail Bloom had no memory of anything that had occurred during the past two days. The shocking dark cloud of amnesia covered a period of time that began, unshockingly, the instant she had stepped into the office of Dr. Fell for her routine physical. She recalled looking back and seeing her mother sink down into Dr. Fell's purple couch to bury herself in the surprisingly convenient copy of *Blimp Enthusiast*, then placing her hand upon the handle of the heavy oak door.

Then nothing.

"Do you even remember opening the door?" asked Jerry.

To which Gail could only shake her head.

"Really? The whole rest of the week?" asked Nancy. "What about Bud Fetidsky's broken leg?"

To which Gail could only shake her head.

Jerry and Nancy did their best to bring their sister and friend up to speed; then the three of them climbed out of the Pinkblossom basement and stepped outside into the oppressive light of day.

No closer to understanding the mystery of Dr. Fell.

Or the danger.

Days passed, as they tend to do when left to themselves. The three children continued to witness blissful emptiness creep into the eyes of children at school, as well as all adults in the area. The fact that Gail, once she had been brought back from the depths, held no memory of her time spent under the spell of Dr. Fell caused the three friends a great deal of concern. What had the ominous man done to Gail while he'd had her under his control? How was his influence spreading so quickly through the neighborhood?

Where would it end?

By now the playground in front of the home of Dr. Fell was littered with children twenty-four hours a day, seven days a week. The children of McKinley Grant Fillmore Elementary School were now joined by the students of Washington Madison Hoover Elementary School, Lincoln Adams Coolidge Elementary School, and even the far-off private elementary school of Southeast North Northwestern Academy, which began running regular bus routes to and from the end of Hardscrabble Street to better serve the needs of its students.

With so many children playing on the structure, the number of accidental injuries naturally increased, as did the number of swift remedies administered by Dr. Fell, as did the number of children mindlessly muttering, "What a nice man is Dr. Fell."

That no parent, teacher, principal, or other adult authority figure had any problem with so many children skipping class, skipping meals, or skipping sleep to play at Dr. Fell's bothered no one at all.

Except for Jerry, Nancy, and Gail.

For the life of them, they could not understand why they, and they alone, had proven more or less immune to Dr. Fell's spell. Certainly, Gail had succumbed for a time, but that had been after receiving personal, one-on-one attention from the so-called good doctor. Many of the children blathering on about the greatness of Dr. Fell nonstop had yet to so much as glimpse the man.

What was it that allowed the three of them to withstand the call? wondered Gail, Nancy, and Jerry.

Gail thought it might have something to do with their tight bonds of friendship. Jerry and Nancy disagreed.

Nancy thought it might have something to do with their general disregard for authority. Gail and Jerry disagreed.

Jerry thought it might have something to do with the molecular resonation of their bodies' atoms. Gail and Nancy had no idea what he was talking about.

All three of them were wrong.

Just under a week after shaking reality back into her best friend's head, Nancy Pinkblossom found herself stomping a few feet behind her mother in the grocery store on a boring Thursday afternoon. She had not wanted to accompany her mother on the mind-numbingly dull errand, but had agreed to go after Cecilia Pinkblossom had promised to take her to the mall afterward and buy her the new shirt Nancy had set her sights upon. It was in the window of Nancy's favorite store, DarkDoom Design, and consisted of a series of Chinese characters advertised to say "Peace to all mankind" but which, she'd been told by the smug clerk in utmost confidence, actually stated, "I'm better than you."

Nancy had to have it.

Mrs. Pinkblossom had not really wanted to bring her daughter along on the errand either, but she had felt a nagging need to try to spend time with Nancy, since she'd read somewhere that that was what parents did with their children. So she'd bribed Nancy with the promise of an inappropriate shirt.

Nancy shuffled her feet as she passed a pyramid of overripe bananas, a display of fresh-baked muffins, and finally Old Lady Witherton, who could not be bothered to get out of the way. She followed doggedly behind her mother, rolling her eyes at no one in particular simply for the practice.

"Do we need cucumbers, Nancy?" asked her mother, as she had asked regarding seemingly each and every item she passed in the store.

"Yes," answered Nancy, who had been saying "yes" every

time the question was posed for no other reason than that it was easier than actually considering the question.

"What about red pepper?"

"Yes."

"Avocados?"

"Yes."

"My goodness, do we have anything left in the fridge?"

"Yes."

"Oh? What?"

Nancy froze, suddenly realizing her lazy, automatic replies had painted her into a corner. "Mustard," she answered, ever quick on her feet.

Satisfied, Cecilia Pinkblossom continued down the aisle, and Nancy breathed a sigh of relief. As her mother returned to her clueless shopping, Nancy's mind returned once again to the dilemma of Dr. Fell. Though she had not spied him in some time, she was certain the man was up to no good. In fact, she was ready to go so far as to call him sinister.

The problem was figuring out just what he was being sinister about.

"Cantaloupe?" asked Mrs. Pinkblossom.

"Yes," answered Nancy.

Dr. Fell seemed determined to be universally beloved, and that was never a good thing. Nancy didn't trust anybody who wanted everyone to like them. It usually meant they were hiding something. Her father had wanted everyone to like him, and he'd certainly been hiding something.

"Scallions?"

"Yes."

So what was Dr. Fell hiding? A secret identity? A dark and twisted past? An abomination living in his dark basement?

"Dr. Fell!"

"Yes. What? No!"

Nancy looked up to find the sinister man smiling at her mother. "A supremely pleasant good afternoon to you, my dear Mrs. Pinkblossom," he purred.

In answer to this utterly predictable greeting, Nancy's mother giggled and blushed, raising her hand in front of her face. Dr. Fell, in turn, smartly ducked his head and tipped his purple top hat. Nancy noticed he seemed much more at ease performing this action than when they had first met. He also seemed to be standing up straighter.

"Why, Dr. Fell, I . . . I didn't expect . . . That is, it's so wonderful to . . . I've never . . ." Mrs. Pinkblossom was at an obvious loss for words.

"Indeed," continued Dr. Fell, as if Cecilia Pinkblossom had just finished a complete sentence. "My occasional agoraphobic tendencies and habitual solitude render a chance encounter within such confines as this sustenance purveyor a wholly unlikely circumstance."

She stared at him, mouth open wide, eyes frozen in confusion.

"What I mean to say is," he continued with a smile, "I do not get out much."

There was a particularly bright twinkle in his eye as he said this, and Nancy got the strange feeling that Dr. Fell was having some fun at her mother's expense.

"Oh! Well, of course I understand," said Mrs. Pinkblossom. "A person is entitled to his privacy. You are such a public figure in our community as it is."

"Quite," agreed Dr. Fell, turning and finally letting his gaze fall on Nancy. "We meet again, my dear urchin."

"You've met my daughter?"

"Of course," replied Dr. Fell. "It was she, along with her two earnest young companions, who was my first introduction to the denizens of this magical hamlet in which I have chosen to live out my remaining days."

"Oh, dear," worried Mrs. Pinkblossom. "Did she insult you? I'm afraid she isn't always the most polite child. I'm so sorry—"

"Not at all, sweet Cecilia," Dr. Fell assured Cecilia without taking his eyes off Nancy. "Your daughter was the picture perfect of virtuous feminine youth."

There was a moment of awkward silence, in which Nancy grew increasingly uneasy under the harsh glare of Dr. Fell's bright white smile.

"That doesn't sound like my Nancy," mumbled Mrs. Pinkblossom. "Are you sure you're thinking of the same girl?"

"You know, Miss Pinkblossom," continued Dr. Fell, taking a leisurely step in Nancy's direction while ignoring her mother completely, "I recently had the pleasure of receiving your dear friend Miss Bloom in my offices for her yearly physical examination."

"Yeah?" Nancy had a nagging fear she knew where this was going.

"I would be most honored to offer my humble services to you and your family toward a similar end," said Dr. Fell, confirming Nancy's suspicions.

"What a wonderful idea!" exclaimed her mother. "You're due for a physical anyway!"

"In two months."

"The early bird catches the worm, Miss Pinkblossom," reasoned Dr. Fell. "You're in a delicate time of development. Your body is undergoing daily readjustments as it pushes forth toward young adulthood. It would be a shame to allow an unforeseen complication to go unobserved for any length of time."

Nancy had so many problems with this, she didn't know where to start. Unfortunately, her mother answered first.

"That is so true, Dr. Fell! Nancy is at such an awkward age. When do you think you could squeeze her in?"

Dr. Fell's face lit up with an earnest, humble, innocent grin that set Nancy's teeth on edge. "Why, I do believe I've an opening tomorrow morning at ten a.m. sharp," he said.

"Perfect!" cheered Cecilia Pinkblossom.

"No!" objected Nancy, drawing the attention not only of her mother and Dr. Fell, but of the two or three nearest grocery shoppers.

"Is there a problem, young urchin?" asked Dr. Fell.

"I . . . can't do it tomorrow," stammered Nancy, her mind in overdrive. "There's a . . . I'm planning on . . . We're learning fractions tomorrow in school, and I've been looking forward to this for . . . a long time."

It was a weak lie, but the best she could come up with under the pressure.

"Fractions?" asked Dr. Fell.

"Oh, yes," replied Nancy, digging herself deeper. "I've always been interested in fractions."

Whether Dr. Fell believed her or not, Nancy couldn't tell, but luckily, her mother believed enough for both of them. "Well now," she said, "I don't think I've ever heard you say you were looking forward to something at school. That's wonderful!"

Nancy nodded, not trusting herself to say anything more.

"Far be it for me to interfere with the unparalleled joy of education," said Dr. Fell. "Consider your appointment rescheduled for Thursday. Ten a.m. sharp. Good day."

And just like that, Nancy's fate was sealed.

Chapter II

The Tragedy at Dr. Fell's

"So you're going to see Dr. Fell?" asked Gail the next morning as she and Nancy went through the motions of playing on Dr. Fell's playground while waiting for the school bus. They had learned some time ago that neglecting to play on the playground first thing in the morning brought forth suspicious looks from the other children.

There were easily more children on the playground each morning than there were students at McKinley Grant Fillmore Elementary School. Bowing to the inevitable, every school within a twenty-mile radius had added the end of Hardscrabble Street to its bus routes. Southeast North

Northwestern Academy had even begun holding classes in one of the playground's turrets.

"Of course I'm not going," assured Nancy. "I'll come up with something tomorrow to get out of it. Knowing my mother, she'll forget about the whole idea in a day or two. Where's your brother?"

Nancy's neck twisted back and forth as she searched for Jerry. Normally, of course, she didn't give a flying flounder fin about the whereabouts of her archnemesis, but things were anything but normal these days. The nerdy third grader was the only one apart from Gail and herself not zombified by Dr. Fell, and she wanted to make sure he stayed that way.

Plus, though she was loath to admit it, a tiny glimmer of respect for him had begun to flicker to life somewhere inside Nancy after they'd rescued Gail together.

"Still at home," answered Gail, who did not bother to twist her neck around. "He said he was working on something but he'd make the bus."

"What is he working on?"

"He wouldn't say."

Their conversation was interrupted by the arrival of three school buses from far-off Ford Garfield Taft Elementary, which always arrived before buses from anywhere else, owing to the thirty-five-minute commute between the playground and the school.

As usual, the arrival of any of the buses was met with a general groan from the students expected to relinquish their time on the playground. Inevitably, a few kids would slink away and hide—often in one of the playground's dungeons or else up in the aviary—but by and large they would fall into line and reluctantly march into the buses, heads drooping in sadness.

On this particular morning, however, one of the students from far-off Ford Garfield Taft Elementary had decided that enough was enough. As his compatriots boarded the bus mindlessly like proverbial lemmings (actual lemmings, it should be noted, do not generally follow one another mindlessly to their doom, despite what you may have heard), the child—whom everyone would very soon know to be eleven-year-old Leonid Hazardfall—climbed to the top of one of the three giant masts of the pirate ship section in the center of the playground and waved a makeshift flag back and forth in the morning breeze.

"Brothers and sisters!" he cried. "We need not blindly obey our elders! Let us, instead, remove the chains of bondage tying us to our education and live out the remainder of our lives in this childhood Eden with which we have been blessed!" Adding to the impact of his words was the fact that he stood bare chested (the flag was his T-shirt) with a zigzag pattern of war paint on his hairless chest.

It was about as imposing a figure as an eleven-year-old could make, and some of his brothers and sisters from Ford Garfield Taft Elementary—as well as many of his cousins, aunts, and uncles from other schools—were ready to give his plan serious thought.

But then Leonid slipped and fell to the ground, landing with a truly sickening thud—but not before slamming into

a dozen different levels and platforms and poles on the way down.

A hush fell over the entire playground. Even the school buses idled just a bit more quietly. The deck of the pirate ship on which Leonid had landed was out of sight of most of the children, yet rather than run forward to his aid, the crowd stood motionless.

Waiting to hear him scream in agony.

Silence.

More waiting.

More silence.

It began to dawn on many that Leonid Hazardfall was not screaming.

Which caused many in the crowd to scream themselves.

Not, however, the children of Hardscrabble Street, Vexington Avenue, Von Burden Lane, and Turnabout Road, who had grown used to sudden and heart-stoppingly violent injuries.

"Somebody should run and get his parents," suggested Gabby Plaugestein.

"Somebody should run and get Dr. Fell," suggested Zachary Fallowmold.

"Somebody should run and play on the playground," suggested Albert Rottingsly. "It's what he would have wanted."

Suddenly everyone had a suggestion, everyone needed everyone else to hear their suggestion, and everyone was telling everyone else that their suggestion was better. What nobody was doing, however, was dealing with the fact that an eleven-year-old classmate had just fallen to what seemed to all to be his death right in front of them.

"This is crazy!" yelled Gail, trying to be heard over the rising cacophony. "We need to call an ambulance!"

"Does anybody have a phone?!" asked Nancy of a gaggle of frantic children. "Did anyone swipe their parents' phone this morning?"

Nobody answered the two girls' call of sanity and clear thinking (though there were, in fact, seven cell phones on-site at that particular moment, three of which had, indeed, been swiped by children from parents that very morning). In fact, the very idea of sanity and clear thinking had been tossed out one of the many stained-glass windows lining the walls of the cathedral section of the play structure. Faced with undeniable tragedy, the crowd of children and bus drivers was descending into absolute chaos.

"Come on!" Gail tugged Nancy's arm, and the two girls raced into the play structure to find Leonid Hazardfall.

As neither of the two had memorized the layout of Dr. Fell's extravagant wonderland (unlike most of the other children, including at least two who had maps of it tattooed onto their bodies), it took Nancy and Gail a few moments of ducking under platforms, climbing over walls, sliding down slides, doubling back upon reaching dead ends, and on one occasion swinging on a rope across a deep chasm. But soon enough they hauled themselves up onto the deck of the wooden ship and found poor Leonid Hazardfall crumpled in a heap at the foot of the ship's wheel.

His body looked like that of a marionette whose puppeteer was attempting to pack it into a small box, with arms and legs bent and folded over on themselves in ways that ought to have had the poor child screaming in agony.

He was not screaming.

He was not moving.

He did not appear to be breathing.

"Oh, no," whispered Gail.

Nancy stepped forward and knelt at the young boy's side. Gingerly, gently, she reached out her hand and felt along his neck.

"What are you doing?" asked Gail.

"Feeling for a pulse," answered Nancy.

There was a pause before Gail—unable to wait any longer—asked, "Well? Do you feel one?"

Gingerly, gently, Nancy withdrew her hand and shook her head. "Nothing," she said.

Both girls choked up, tears silently flowing down their cheeks as they stared at the lifeless body in front of them.

"Dear me, dear me indeed. Has one of the charming munchkins availing themselves of my largesse suffered a frightening accident?"

Nancy and Gail lifted their heads to find Dr. Fell standing on the deck of the sailing ship play structure. He took a sip of yellow liquid from a navy-blue glass through a teal-colored straw, smiled his friendly smile, and reached up with a steady hand (and a bit of a flourish) to tip his purple top hat in greeting.

"Accident?" asked Nancy. "He's dead!"

"Nonsense!" scoffed Dr. Fell, approaching the horrifyingly mangled Leonid Hazardfall. "It would be most impolite for the lad to shuffle off this mortal coil within the confines of my monument to youthful frivolity. Let's have ourselves a look, shall we?"

Dr. Fell knelt down on one knee, setting his glass aside for the moment, and inspected the broken and battered body of Leonid Hazardfall.

"He doesn't have a pulse!" said Nancy.

"Indeed," mumbled Dr. Fell, remaining focused on the body before him. "How astute of you to notice."

He grunted to himself once as he felt the boy's forehead, grunted again as he felt the boy's neck, and grunted a third time as he placed both hands on the boy's chest.

"He's dead! Dead!"

"Rubbish," remarked Dr. Fell. "I do not mean to be rude, young lady, but I believe only one of us here has the medical training necessary to make that rather final declaration on the boy's behalf."

With a deep breath to steady himself, Dr. Fell slipped his arms beneath poor Leonid Hazardfall's body and gently lifted him off the ground.

"My sincerest apologies to you, my good urchins, for your having to witness this unforeseen tragedy," he said. "It is a shame that young and impressionable minds such as yours should view firsthand the result of such a devastating descent from atop the crow's nest. However, while the young man does appear to be in unquestionably bad shape, I assure you that his injuries are not life threatening. Please do carry on frolicking within the friendly confines of my magnanimous gift until such a time as you are required to venture forth to school."

He bowed his head to them once again.

"Are you kidding me?!" screamed Nancy.

"On the contrary," replied Dr. Fell, warmth beaming from his face. "I am steadfastly serious. Now if you will excuse me, I need to shepherd this poor boy into the nurturing confines of my medical examination room and tend to his wounds. Be a good lass and hand me my beverage, would you?"

Nancy glared at Dr. Fell, who smiled right back at her. After a moment, Gail picked up the glass and handed it to Dr. Fell, who adjusted the unmoving body of Leonid Hazardfall in his arms until he had a free hand available to hold his drink.

Then he turned and carried the boy away.

Gail and Nancy continued to stare after him in shock long after he had ducked under a platform and disappeared.

"The only reason that kid's injuries aren't life threatening is that he doesn't have any life left to threaten," said Nancy.

"Are you sure?" asked Gail. "I mean, you're not a doctor. Maybe—"

Nancy turned and stopped her. "He had no pulse. He wasn't breathing. He wasn't moving. There isn't a single doubt in my mind."

She turned back to the platform under which Dr. Fell had carried Leonid Hazardfall, saying only, "That boy is dead."

Chapter 12

Jerry's Plan to Expose Dr. Fell

SCHOOL THAT FRIDAY WAS a somber affair. Though Leonid Hazardfall did not attend McKinley Grant Fillmore Elementary School, had no friends there, and had never even heard of it (schools were not discussed on the playground of Dr. Fell), the children at McKinley Grant Fillmore Elementary School nevertheless felt a strong kinship with the poor boy because of their shared love of all things Dr. Fell.

The teachers and administrators of McKinley Grant Fillmore Elementary School knew right away that something was wrong. When the truth came slithering out of hundreds of downturned mouths, a wave of relief spread across the staff due to the fact that the injured and possibly dead child was not one of theirs and also that Dr. Fell himself was unharmed and the play structure undamaged.

Jerry took the news of the boy's fall particularly hard, and unfortunately, neither Gail nor Nancy was in a position to cheer him up, as they, too, were profoundly devastated.

"You really think he's dead?" he asked yet again as the three sat in the corner of the lunchroom, having quarantined themselves away from the seemingly rabid pack of Dr. Fell cultists.

"Trust me," answered Nancy yet again. "There's no way that boy survived that fall. He probably broke every bone in his body on the way down."

"So I'm too late," Jerry mumbled once again.

"All right, that's it," said Gail. "Either tell us what you mean or quit saying that."

"What?" objected Jerry. "I didn't say any—"

"Stuff it, Dorknose," interrupted Nancy, while she silently wondered how Dorknose—one of her weaker insults—had become her go-to taunt when she was stressed. "Start talking."

Jerry opened his mouth to protest but then gave up and slumped back down into his chair.

"Well?" prompted his sister.

He looked quickly left and right, then leaned forward and spoke in an almost whisper. "I'm working on a way to prove Dr. Fell is not what he says he is."

"You mean like a space alien or something?" asked Nancy in a sarcastic tone far too loud for Jerry's liking.

"Will you keep it down?" He waved his hands toward the table to illustrate "keeping it down."

"Oh, come on, Dorknose!"

"I'm serious!" seethed Jerry through his teeth. "Everybody at school's a Felligan!"

Nancy scrunched up her eyebrows in confusion. "A what?" she asked.

"You know. Dr. Fell . . . hooligan. Felligan."

Nancy snorted through her nose.

"They really aren't so much hooligans as zombies," commented Gail.

"Yeah, but Fellombie doesn't really work," admitted Jerry. "Neither does Fultists or Fellultists if you try to call them all cultists. Trust me, I went through all the possibilities."

"And you wonder why you don't have any friends," muttered Nancy.

"Look, the point is," continued Jerry, choosing to ignore her tease, "you can't say anything bad about Dr. Fell at school. Am I right?"

The girls nodded—Nancy somewhat reluctantly, but she had to admit he was right.

"So we need to keep this quiet. And no, I don't think he's a space alien."

He stopped talking as two giggling girls walked by, paying no attention to the three conspirators at all. In fact, they seemed so incredibly uninterested in Nancy, Gail, and Jerry that all three children had the uncomfortable feeling they were being watched.

"Go on," whispered Nancy once the two girls had taken a seat a few tables away. "What are you thinking, then?"

Jerry allowed himself a brief smile and nodded at Nancy in acknowledgment of her whisper. "I think he built the playground to lure kids to his house so that they get injured and he gets rich."

The girls stared at him, ready to laugh him off but not quite able to dismiss his theory.

"How, exactly?" asked Gail.

"Yeah, he generally doesn't charge when he fixes up a scrape or a cut or whatever," said Nancy.

"No, but how many kids have been seeing him for regular checkups? Those aren't free."

"I dunno," said Nancy. "It seems a little too simple."

"Grown-ups are always simple!" countered Jerry. With which neither girl could disagree.

"But what about Bud Fetidsky's leg?" asked Gail.

This was a puzzle, and Jerry didn't have an answer. Finally, he shrugged. "Maybe it really wasn't as bad as we thought it was," he admitted.

The three children stewed on this for a moment, each trying to make sense out of the seeming impossibility of Bud Fetidsky's miraculous healing powers.

"All right, Dorknose," said Nancy. "What's your plan? How are you going to prove your theory?"

"I'm not," said Jerry. Both girls were about to protest, but he held up his hand. "I just don't think it's something we can prove. But I do have a plan to stop him."

He heaved his backpack up onto the table and pulled

out two large, dusty books more likely to be used to frighten children than actually to be read. With as minimal a flourish as possible (and a quick glance to see if the two girls at the other table were paying attention—they weren't), he opened one of the massive tomes and flipped forward through the volume until he came to a candy wrapper crammed into the spine between two pages.

"What in the world is that?" asked Gail.

Jerry looked up and smiled. "City building codes," he answered. He then placed his finger midway on the page and read aloud. "Any external structure measuring a quarter again the square footage of half the total acreage contained within the nominal residence of the property shall adhere to all laws and regulations pursuant to human habitation or else be summarily removed pending certain litigation."

He looked up at them, beaming.

"I didn't understand a single word of that," said Nancy.

"There was half of something in there, right?" asked Gail. "You said the word 'half.' "

"Yeah, I didn't get it at first either. But I asked the librarian to explain, and it's actually pretty simple. What it means," said Jerry, grinning from ear to ear, "is that Dr. Fell's playground cannot possibly have been built legally. If that's true, it will be torn down. By law. All I have to do is take some measurements today after school, and Dr. Fell's little get-rich-quick scheme is over."

Nancy and Gail shared a look that surprised them both. They liked the plan. It was a good plan. It would work. All that was left was to visit the playground after school and let

Jerry take his measurements, and they would give Dr. Fell the surprise of his life.

But when school ended and they followed the throng of eager children toward the beckoning paradise of the play structure, the surprise of their young lives was already waiting for them.

High atop the crow's nest, waving his shirt back and forth like a flag and shouting "Argh, mateys!" was the decidedly not-dead Leonid Hazardfall.

Chapter 13

The Second Miracle of Dr. Fell

LEONID HAZARDFALL WAS HEAVILY bruised, his left arm was wrapped in bandages, and he wore a large padded brace around his neck, but he was most certainly very much alive.

The horde of children emerging from school buses cheered with relief at the sight of their fellow playground enthusiast. The race to the playground became a stampede as the undeniable evidence of the boy's miraculous recovery allowed them all once again to put their unshakable faith into the playground of Dr. Fell.

"I'm gonna go scale the mini Eiffel Tower!" announced a young boy from Washington Madison Hoover Elementary School.

"I'm gonna go play inside the ice castle!" announced a young girl from Lincoln Adams Coolidge Elementary School.

"I'm gonna go crawl through the catacombs!" announced an older boy from Southeast North Northwestern Academy.

Standing their ground as the stampede of happy children charged past, Gail, Nancy, and Jerry could only gawk at the shocking sight of Leonid Hazardfall being shockingly not dead.

"That's amazing," said Gail.

"That's impossible," said Jerry.

"That's seriously wrong," said Nancy.

"Isn't it great that the kid's all right?" asked the ever-perky Jewel Sparkledink as she ran past them.

"But he was dead!" Nancy called after her.

"Don't be silly—he just had a bad fall," said the only slightly less perky Shelly Plentyson as she followed in Jewel Sparkledink's footsteps.

"He had no pulse!" pointed out Nancy in disbelief.

"So?" said impossibly perky Crystal Chintzington as she raced after Shelly Plentyson and Jewel Sparkledink. "He saw Dr. Fell, so of course he's OK!"

Soon the flood of eager children washed past them, leaving the three alone on the sidewalk. Despite the invisible force drawing them toward the playground like a magnet, they held their ground a moment longer.

"I'm telling you, that kid was dead," said Nancy. "I swear it. D-E-A-D dead."

"Maybe it was a . . . you know . . . pulled-back-from-the-afterlife sort of thing," suggested Gail. "What's it called? When you die and then come back?"

"Reincarnation," replied Jerry helpfully.

"Right! Maybe he's reincarnated."

"Except when you're reincarnated, you come back as something else, like a cockroach or a squirrel," clarified Jerry.

"I'd sooner believe he's a zombie," said Nancy. "They come back from the dead too."

Jerry and Gail's silence showed they weren't about to disagree.

Behind them, another fleet of school buses arrived to vomit out the children of Ford Garfield Taft Elementary. The students immediately spotted their no-longer-dead classmate standing atop the mast and cheered.

"Look!" cried one little boy. "It's Leonid!"

"Look!" cried another boy. "He's alive!"

"Look!" cried a little girl. "The playground is still awesome!"

The doors of the buses opened and children ran into the waiting arms of the play structure, which swallowed them up like some diabolical children-eating sponge.

"I'm scared," admitted Jerry.

Nancy nodded, but Gail, ever the optimist, turned to her friends with a forced grin. "I'm sure there's a simple explanation," she said. "Let's go ask him."

"What?" asked Nancy.

"Let's talk to that kid and find out what really happened."

Without waiting for a reply, Gail marched determinedly

toward the ominous play structure of Dr. Fell. Jerry and Nancy silently fell into step behind her.

The buzz of excited children assaulted their ears as they crossed the boundary separating the playground from the rest of reality. Suddenly they were walking through Ethel Pusster's all-you-can-eat sandcake party, then climbing over Aiden Grand and Zachary Fallowmold's deadly wall of man-eating ivy, then crawling through a tunnel that three kids from Lincoln Adams Coolidge Elementary had turned into an abandoned mine shaft, before finally dodging six or seven wall ball players from Southeast North Northwestern Academy and reaching the wooden schooner atop whose central mast stood Leonid Hazardfall in full look-at-me-not-be-dead! glory. They quickly scrambled over the side and pulled themselves up onto the deck.

"Hey!" called out Gail in the universal language of preteens. "Hey, kid!"

Leonid looked down at the three of them, eyes wide with youthful abandon. "Tallyho!" he cried before leaping out into the air, grabbing one of the ropes meant to resemble rigging, and twirling to the ground with his legs kicked out dramatically behind him. All in all, it was a ridiculously dangerous move for a recently dead child to undertake.

He landed in a sprightly way in front of them and bowed. "Welcome, ye hearty maidens!" he cried before turning to Jerry. "And cabin boy!"

Gail couldn't help but giggle a bit at Leonid's flair. Nancy rolled her eyes and elbowed her aside. "What are you doing?" she asked, getting straight to the point. "You were dead, like, what? Five hours ago?"

"More like eight," offered Jerry.

"Fine. Eight hours ago. How are you out here now, champing at the bit and being all piratey?"

"Bah!" Leonid waved his hand in front of his face as if he were swatting a fly. "'Twas but a flesh wound!"

"You weren't breathing!"

Leonid stopped, and for a moment, a look of clarity pushed its way through his pirate shtick. "What do you mean?" he asked.

"I was there! You weren't breathing! You had no pulse! You were dead!"

Behind Nancy, Gail and Jerry nodded their support for Leonid being dead.

"Well . . . well . . ." Leonid Hazardfall appeared to be at a loss. Finally, he shrugged. "Well, I'm all better now!"

He squeaked out the last word, his voice cracking. He instinctively covered his mouth in embarrassment.

"You OK?" asked Gail.

The formerly dead eleven-year-old dropped his arms to his sides and shrugged. "Dr. Fell made me all be-eh-ter." The two-syllable word became three as his voice once again cracked on the vowel.

"Why are you doing that?" asked an irritated Nancy.

"Doing what?"

"That thing with your voice."

"I'm not do-oo-ing anything." He forced the words through his breaking voice.

Nancy scowled. Gail looked concerned. Jerry stared off into space, concentrating.

"Avast!" yelled Leonid, once again in character. "Landlubbers, beware!" With that, he dashed off to find some landlubbers to conquer.

"That was weird," said Gail.

"That was disturbing," said Jerry.

"That was lame," said Nancy.

"Why, if it is not my three favorite urchins! A supremely pleasant good afternoon to you all," purred the pleasing voice of Dr. Fell. The children turned to find the good doctor slightly hunched over behind them, sipping his usual drink from an aquamarine glass through a honeydew-colored straw. He was dressed once again in his blacker-than-black old-fashioned suit despite it being a hot day with clear skies. Though he stood out in the open, he was almost completely in shadow thanks to his bright purple top hat, which shaded him (in an almost unnatural way) from the blazing sun overhead. "It brings me no small amount of gratification to chance upon the three of you—who have heretofore managed such complete avoidance of my generosity—displaying an unbridled joy within the confines of this magical nook."

He smiled widely and easily dipped the front of his hat, as he always did, before continuing. "What I mean to say is—"

"We know what you meant to say," interrupted Nancy, who had actually been stumped by a couple of the bigger words but wasn't about to admit it. "We're not stupid."

Dr. Fell froze. It was only a fraction of a second, but

they all saw it, and it made them all shiver in terror. A moment later, Dr. Fell regained his composure and smiled even more widely. "Of course not. Please forgive me, Miss Pinkblossom. I was simply striving for clarity."

"Excuse me?" asked a very hesitant Gail. "Dr. Fell?"

Dr. Fell somehow managed to turn his attention to Gail without taking his eyes off Nancy. It was both remarkable and unnerving. "Yes, Miss Bloom?"

Gail stepped forward, very purposefully, in front of Nancy. She knew just how short her friend's fuse could be and felt the need to intervene before an explosion occurred. "We were wondering . . . What did you . . . It's just that . . ." She frowned. She knew what she wanted to ask but for some reason was unable to put her thought into words. Instead, she simply pointed up at the overly active Leonid Hazardfall and said, simply, "How?"

Dr. Fell took a long, slow sip of yellow liquid. Gail, Nancy, and Jerry waited patiently for him to finish. Finally, with a sickly satisfied sigh, he lowered the glass.

"How did I bring him back from the dead?"

A chill colder than ice shook the three children to their core. Their eyes widened, their hearts raced, and sweat oozed out of their pores.

Then Dr. Fell laughed. It was not an evil someday-I'm-going-to-rule-the-world laugh, but rather a good-natured I-can't-believe-you-fell-for-that laugh.

"Oh, I am sorry, my little lovelies, but I simply could not resist a stroke of merriment at the expense of your overly eager imaginations. Young Mr. Hazardfall took quite the spill, indeed, but he merely had the wind knocked out of him. As you can obviously see, he is none the worse for wear, with the exception of a few bumps and bruises."

"No way!" Nancy spun out of her daze with a vengeance. "He wasn't breathing! He didn't have a pulse!"

"I must disagree with your medical diagnosis. I assure you, the young man gave us a scare, nothing more. His injuries, though dramatic, were no match for my medical prowess. He shall live to dance a jig on his wedding day!" At this he danced a little jig, ending by kicking up his heels in a moment of extreme silliness.

The three children tried not to laugh.

"Whew! I am not the young man I once was," he said, pulling a white monogrammed handkerchief from his coat pocket and dabbing his forehead. "Now, if you will excuse me, I must continue my rounds, as it were. It has been an absolute pleasure speaking with you all."

He stuffed the handkerchief back in his pocket.

"Miss Pinkblossom, I look forward to our appointment tomorrow. Ten a.m. sharp."

They watched him slink away into the forest of children that suddenly seemed to be running willy-nilly all around them. In the blink of an eye, it seemed, he was gone.

"That was also disturbing," said Jerry.

Gail turned to Nancy, a look of concern etched on her face. "Do you think you can convince your mother to cancel your appointment with him?" she asked.

Nancy's eyes narrowed into battle formation, and her notorious scowl settled onto her face. "No, but I wouldn't even if I could. I'm keeping that appointment," she announced. "I'm going to walk into the lion's den and figure out just what Dr. Fell is up to."

Chapter 14

Nancy's Appointment with Dr. Fell

THE NEXT MORNING, NANCY prepared herself for the day's appointment. Although she felt she would be better able to fend off the spell of Dr. Fell than her friend had been, she had still taken precautions. The basement was once again set up for an "exorcism," complete with chair and rope and single lightbulb; and Gail and Jerry had promised to hang her upside down and shake her back to reality if she fell under the man's spell.

As she wolfed down her breakfast cereal, Nancy tried to figure out how Dr. Fell was doing whatever it was he was doing. She wanted to be ready for any possibility. He was too frail and weak to be physically overpowering anyone (though she had to admit he didn't seem quite as fragile as he had when they'd first met him). She supposed he could be injecting people with some weird, freaky serum while telling them it was a flu shot or a vaccine, but if that was the case, then she simply wouldn't let him inject anything into her. And she wouldn't eat or drink anything he offered her either. Another possibility was that he was hypnotizing his victims, so she practiced slamming her eyelids shut at a moment's notice—she was pretty sure you couldn't be hypnotized when your eyes were closed.

She got a little worried about the possibility that he was pumping some sort of crazy gas into the examination room. She couldn't exactly wear a gas mask during her visit without arousing his suspicions, and she couldn't really hold her breath for very long. But then she figured that if Dr. Fell were using gas, he'd be gassing himself, too, and that didn't make any sense.

And if she saw him slipping a gas mask on, she'd just run out of the room.

She was in the midst of considering what to do in case Dr. Fell had some sort of strange mind powers (could she get away with wearing a tinfoil hat to the appointment?) when Cecilia Pinkblossom came downstairs and gasped with a start.

"Nancy? You're . . . you're going to go to your appointment with Dr. Fell this morning?" asked her mother.

"Of course," answered Nancy, trying to be as sweet and good-daughterly as possible. "Why wouldn't I?"

"Well . . . I mean . . . ," sputtered Mrs. Pinkblossom,

obviously a bit flustered. "You never do anything I tell you to do."

Nancy frowned. This was true, and it had never occurred to her that she'd raise suspicions by doing what she was told. "Well," she reasoned, "I already put it off a day with that whole 'I care about fractions' lie, so, I mean, I may as well get it over with."

Her mother sagged a bit, saddened to learn that her daughter did not, in fact, care about fractions. "Oh," she replied, dejected. "Oh, that's too bad."

"Yeah, I mean, everyone else has seen the guy, right?"

"Yes, of course. I simply assumed you'd rebel against the idea and run off to school instead. That's why I asked Assistant Principal Richman to arrange for some of the janitorial staff to kidnap you at nine-thirty this morning and bring you to your appointment kicking and screaming if need be." She frowned as if just thinking of something. "I really should call Assistant Principal Richman and tell him his help won't be needed after all."

She scurried from the room to find her phone, leaving Nancy alone with the remnants of her soggy cereal.

Cecilia Pinkblossom lived to be punctual. Normally that would be reason enough for Nancy to be late, but today she just wanted to get in there and get this over with. So it was that at 9:59 a.m., the two stood on Dr. Fell's porch, Mrs. Pinkblossom's right hand ready to knock on the front door while her eyes rested on the watch on her left wrist.

"Just knock already," groaned Nancy.

Mrs. Pinkblossom hushed her daughter, and the two

stood in silence a few moments more until the second hand reached twelve and she moved to knock.

The door opened a fraction of a second before her knuckles could make contact.

"My heart leaps with the syncopated beats of gaiety to meet a kindred spirit with regard to the necessity of precise punctuality," said Dr. Fell from within. "I do fear this antiquated nicety has egregiously fallen from favor since the days of my own schooling."

He stood in the doorway, an imposingly towering figure all in the shadow of his purple top hat, which really didn't seem large enough to be casting so much darkness. It was almost as if the light went out of its way to avoid touching Dr. Fell. For an instant, Nancy's fight-or-flight instinct roared to life, warning her to get as far away from this dangerous predator as possible.

Then he flashed his smile, and the instinct was swept away by warm fuzzies.

"Oh! Dr. Fell!" stammered Cecilia Pinkblossom. "I am . . . That is . . ."

"What I mean to say," continued Dr. Fell without skipping a beat, "is—"

"You're glad we're on time," snapped Nancy. "We get it. Can we get on with this?"

Dr. Fell's eyes laughed even while the rest of him remained calm. "But of course," he replied, stepping back from the doorway and politely gesturing for them to enter.

Nancy pushed her way past her mother and into the home of Dr. Fell. The room was every bit as freaky as Gail had described. She'd never seen so much purple in one place. It dazzled her from every corner, every nook and cranny, every surface. It was like some big, ugly, purple goo monster had exploded inside Dr. Fell's living room and splattered its purple guts in every direction.

And then there were the cats.

Gail had talked about all the portraits of kittens, but she hadn't done the room justice. There were pictures of cats—both kittens and older cats—taking up every available inch of wall space. A kitten dressed as an astronaut stared at her next to an older cat dressed as a ballet dancer next to two kittens dressed up to look like elephants. Portraits even hung from the ceiling, with one overly crowded picture depicting what looked like an all-feline baseball team taking the field. Nancy recognized some of the pictures from Gail's description—there was the kitten drinking milk, there were the kittens lying on beds—though they looked more like regular cats than kittens. Above the fireplace was the cat dressed like a clown—it actually appeared quite old and seemed to be losing its fur—frowning out at the room as if it did not approve of all the other cats and kittens present.

"You really have a thing for cats, don't you, Dr. Fell?" she asked.

"On the contrary," replied Dr. Fell. "I cannot abide the filthy creatures. Now then, can I offer either of you an apple?"

Nancy jerked around, instantly alert, to find Dr. Fell holding a plate of bright-red apples. Nancy's mother loved apples. Absolutely loved them.

"I love apples!" squealed her mother with delight. "Absolutely love them!"

She took the plate from Dr. Fell and descended upon the apples like a lion digging into a fresh carcass on the African savanna. "Jeez, Mom," murmured Nancy. "Slow down—they're not going anywhere."

"Theeth arr the bethst appllleth in thhh world!" cheered Cecilia Pinkblossom, somehow managing to speak, bite, chew, and swallow all at the same time.

"I am so very pleased you find them to your liking, Madam Pinkblossom," said Dr. Fell, turning his attention to the younger Pinkblossom. "And now, my sweet young Pinkblossom. Shall we begin?"

He gestured with a straight, firm hand to the dark, stout oak door Gail had mentioned. Nancy had to agree with her: she didn't remember that door being in the house when it had been vacant. A rather sad poster of two elderly cats trying to dance *The Nutcracker* had been pinned to the door in an attempt to unify it with the rest of the room. The effect, however, was less than successful. There was something very, very off about this eerily dark, solid door. It was an imposter. An artifact from another time and place that most certainly had no business being there.

Nancy did not want to go through it.

"I'm not getting any shots," she said defiantly, though in truth more to put off approaching the door than from any implied upcoming vaccinations.

"Duly noted," said Dr. Fell.

"And I'm not drinking anything. Or eating anything."

"Is that simply for the duration of your examination, or do you intend to commence upon a hunger strike?"

He smiled down at her pleasantly. She glared right back up at him and was momentarily taken aback by how much taller he seemed to be now that he was no longer so hunched over. In fact, he didn't seem to be hunched over at all anymore. Which was strange.

What was going on with this guy? What was his secret? What was he after? She mentally went through her anti-Felligan checklist, making sure she hadn't forgotten anything. She couldn't take any chances; she had to get in there and stay Nancy rather than become zombie-Nancy.

"All right," she said finally. "Let's get this over with."

He nodded, his hand never having wavered from its invitation. "Youthful possibility before ancient finality," he said, which she figured was just his crazy way of saying "After you."

Confident she was prepared for whatever was coming, Nancy held her head high, walked forward, pushed the dark, stout oak door open, and entered the strange doctor's lair.

Chapter 15

The Diabolical Cunning of Dr. Fell

THAT AFTERNOON, AFTER GAIL and Jerry had tied Nancy to the chair in her basement, turned her upside down, and shaken free will back into her, the three kids sat outside on Nancy's porch, staring down the block at the heaving throng of children gathered on the play structure in front of Dr. Fell's house.

Still shivering after her return to normalcy, Nancy quietly sipped a juice box, letting Gail and Jerry do most of the talking.

"Seriously? You don't remember anything?" asked Jerry.

"Leave her alone, Jerry," said Gail. "It's not her fault."

"But why do you guys keep blacking out the exact

moment you enter that room? There must be a scientific explanation."

The girls didn't have a scientific explanation, so the three friends sat quietly a moment more, their silence broken by the static-like roar of the children at the end of the street.

"Did I say it?" asked Nancy finally.

"Say what?" asked Jerry right back.

But Gail understood. She lowered her gaze to the ground and nodded. A single tear rolled quietly down Nancy's cheek, followed by a second.

"It's not your fault, Nancy," reassured Gail. "You know that."

More tears followed the first two as Nancy looked back at her best friend in desperation, saying, "I thought I'd be stronger." Gail just put an arm around her friend and let her cry on her shoulder.

"What?" asked an increasingly worried Jerry. "What are you guys talking about? Say what?"

"Think, Jerry," snapped Gail. "What do they all say?"

And Jerry understood.

" 'What a nice man is Dr. Fell,' " he whispered, giving voice to the seven simple words that now struck fear into their hearts.

Once Nancy heard the words aloud, her silent cry evolved into one of sound.

Her inability to withstand the mesmerizing aura of Dr. Fell shot a sudden urgency into Jerry's plan to expose the unnerving old man (who, they all agreed, seemed not quite as expressly old as he had weeks before). They swung by the

House of Bloom to allow Jerry to gather needed supplies, before putting on their blank faces and journeying into the Neverland of Dr. Fell's playground.

As usual, the structure was swarming with innocent youth, each playing to their heart's content. The flow of children over the structure's platforms and poles and ladders and bridges was so complete, it was like a layer of skin stretched over the wooden entity—giving it a life of its own. The effect was so profound that for a moment, Gail, Nancy, and Jerry could almost see it breathing.

Gail was the first to clear the illusion from her mind. "OK, Jerry. Where do we start?"

The eight-year-old self-appointed building inspector furrowed his eyebrows in concentration, envisioning the best way to tackle the enormous task in front of him. Finally, he sighed and took out his tape measure, saying, "I guess we start measuring."

For the next half hour, they worked as a well-oiled machine. They'd move into an area, Nancy would growl away whoever happened by, Jerry would whip his tape measure around, yelling out things like "Left wall! Six feet, three inches high! Open pit! Four feet square! Rope ladder! Twenty-five-inch rungs!" and Gail would jot down everything her brother said.

In this way they tackled in turn the amphitheater/roller rink, the star fighter cockpit, the undersea ruins, and the seedy streets of 1865 London. All the while Nancy kept growling, Jerry kept measuring, and Gail kept jotting. Some of the kids paused in their play to look questioningly at the trio, but Nancy would inevitably shoo them off, and for the most part they were allowed to work in peace.

As the minutes passed and Gail's notebook filled up with numbers, something else came over the three friends. A distinct and palpable feeling of alarm.

They had never actually spent a lot of time on or in the play structure before, or at least not at a time when all three had their wits about them. Before, whenever they'd crossed over into the fanciful atmosphere at the end of Hardscrabble Street, they'd been very singularly focused—first on zombie Gail and then on miraculously not-dead Leonid Hazardfall. Now, however, they studied the structure itself and heard the laughs, shouts, and simple conversations of those cavorting within.

Which led to their heightened state of alarm.

Because beyond the various games or forms of play undertaken by the children, the number one topic of conversation was a rather gleeful recounting of just how many times each child had injured himself or herself on the play structure. It was almost as if the more times you hurt yourself, the more popular you became. Albert Rottingsly was heard boasting that he'd dislocated his shoulder, sprained his ankle, scraped the skin off his knee, and suffered a concussion all within the last week. Shelly Plentyson couldn't stop talking about how she'd sliced open her jaw and fractured all the bones in her left hand on the same day. And Leonid Hazardfall (whose voice was now a deep baritone) had already not-suffered through a series of scrapes, snaps, and bloodings in the single day since his miraculous very-near-death experience.

"This is a very dangerous playground," commented Gail as Jerry measured the drop from the drawbridge down to the dirt moat at the entrance to Fantasy Castle.

"You have to be nuts to play on this thing," agreed Nancy.

"Why do parents let their kids play here?" asked Gail.

"You mean, why do parents actively encourage their kids to play here, don't you?" asked Jerry. "Four feet, seven inches from bridge to moat."

Gail dutifully copied the numbers down.

"Hey! Are you guys done yet?" asked a boy in a deep voice. None of the children recognized him, though Gail thought she might have seen him getting off the bus from Washington Madison Hoover Elementary School earlier that day.

"Go away," snarled Nancy.

The kid, who looked to be perhaps a year or two older than Gail and Nancy, took an involuntary step back but then held his ground. "We kind of need to storm the castle, and you're kind of ruining our play," he said.

"I'm almost done," said Jerry as he tried to measure the imposing height of the castle walls by shoving the end of his tape measure up the side. Unfortunately, it was so high that his tape measure kept flopping back down and he was unable to get an accurate reading.

"Yeah? Well, hurry it up. Me and my buddy are gonna scale those walls and surprise the orcs on the other side."

Jerry's tape measure flopped back down once more. He grumbled and tried again.

"You're going to climb these walls?" asked Gail.

"Totally!" replied the young boy, absently scratching at a small layer of stubble on his cheek.

"But they're so high!" worried Gail.

"At least twenty feet," agreed Jerry, "but I can't get an accurate measurement. I think I need to get up there and measure from the top down."

"Twenty feet!" said Gail. "What if you fall?" she asked the boy.

"We fall all the time. It's no biggie."

"You're lucky you don't break your neck," said Nancy.

"Oh, I have. Twice," said the boy. "But Dr. Fell always fixes me up. So, like, what do you need? Another minute?"

Gail and Nancy and Jerry just stared at the boy in a mixture of wonder and horror. Finally, Jerry nodded. The boy, satisfied, gave a thumbs-up, turned, and ran back the way he'd come.

"He broke his neck?" asked Gail.

"Twice," corrected Jerry.

"I'm no doctor, but shouldn't he be paralyzed? Or dead?"

"So should Leonid Hazardfall," Jerry reminded them.

"How old do you guys think that kid was?" asked Nancy, joining the conversation.

"I'd say maybe eleven or twelve," said Jerry.

"He had stubble," said Nancy. "Like he was growing a beard."

"OK, then maybe he's older. Like fifteen or sixteen."

"He can't be. He goes to Washington Madison Hoover Elementary," pointed out Gail. "That's a K-six school. So he's twelve at the most."

"Huh," said Nancy.

"Huh," said Jerry.

"Huh," said Gail.

"I was unaware that children of your generation found enjoyment in domicile-improvement scenarios. I am forever enriched by the never-ending multitude of imaginations that have descended upon my humble abode."

They didn't have to turn around to know that Dr. Fell had somehow appeared out of nowhere yet again. They didn't have to turn around to know he was standing in the sun yet somehow completely in the shadow of his purple top hat. They didn't have to see him to know that he was smiling his pleasant, innocent, inviting smile on his pleasant, innocent, inviting face.

But they turned around all the same.

"Though I must admit that I am somewhat baffled by your choice of location for such wholesome play," continued Dr. Fell. "I would have thought the condominiums or the model home would be a more practical and appropriate place to entertain fantasies of structural renovation."

"We . . . um . . . ," stammered Gail.

"Oh, please, do not mind me, little urchins. I am simply here to post a copy of the building permit, which I have been neglecting to display. I want parents to know that their own city inspectors have blessed our childhood utopia as being completely safe. I wouldn't want anyone to worry. I'm sure you understand, Mr. Bloom."

His smile grew so wide, it seemed to split his face in two, and Jerry felt a sliver of darkness worm its way into his heart at the mention of his name.

"I . . . I . . . ," he sputtered.

"I am so exceedingly pleased that you agree," said Dr. Fell.

As the three stood, transfixed, Dr. Fell whipped out a small hammer and twirled it around his fingers with one hand while displaying a plastic sheath holding an official-looking document in the other. He held the sheath up against the wall of the castle, then quickly hammered four small finishing nails into its four corners.

"There we are," he said. "Now there is no need for anyone to worry or wonder whether or not my monument to childhood frivolity is properly up to code."

There was a glint in his eye that caused all three children to flinch.

"Now then. I trust the fine trio before me will continue their regalement within the friendly confines of the youthful garden of delights in which they find themselves."

As he had intended, the children continued to stare in silence.

"What I mean to say is . . . have fun on my playground."

A sudden scream of pain echoed from somewhere deep within the structure. Dr. Fell stood up straight and tall and winked. "Ah. I believe my services are required. Good day."

He backed up through the castle gateway, one hand tipping his top hat with a fanciful and unnecessary flick of the wrist, and instantly disappeared into the vast labyrinthine structure he had created.

The paralyzing effect of his presence remained a moment more. Finally, Jerry shook his head clear and raced to the document posted on the castle wall.

"Is it just me, or does that guy get creepier and creepier by the day?" asked Nancy, slapping her face to bring herself out of the spell.

"It's not just you," confirmed Gail, rubbing the bridge of her nose.

"I don't believe it!" said Jerry. "It's all legally approved!"

"That means it's safe, then, right?" asked Gail. "I mean, if the town building inspectors—"

"It's not safe, Gail! The forest of sharp wooden spikes alone should get this thing condemned."

Gail and Nancy joined Jerry and scanned the document themselves, though neither one had any real idea of what they were looking at.

"It just doesn't make any sense!" complained Jerry.

"What's this written here at the bottom?" asked Gail, pointing.

The three kids leaned in to peer at the fine print. Then they read it. Then they sagged.

" 'What a nice man is Dr. Fell,' " read Gail.

"So much for your brilliant plan," grunted Nancy.

Jerry whirled, hurt, but before he could respond, a new understanding dawned on him.

"You told him," he whispered.

"What?" asked Nancy.

"You told him my plan. When he zombified you."

"Don't be stupid."

"He knew it was my plan! He singled me out!"

"You're the one holding the tape measure, Dorknose."

"You told him it was my plan and he went out and bedazzled the building inspector and now everything is ruined! Now we'll never get rid of him!"

"I didn't tell him!"

"You don't know that, Nancy," said Gail. "You'll never know what you did or didn't do when you were under his spell."

"Or maybe you weren't even under his spell yet. Maybe you were jealous that I had the plan to save the day, so you warned him even before he put the heebie-jeebies on you!"

"Come off it, Dorknose. You know I didn't—"

"Then why'd he know it was my plan?! Why'd he single me out?!"

"I don't know!" yelled Nancy, her blood boiling.

"You traitor!" screamed Jerry as he lunged at Nancy, fists flying. Not being the most agile of individuals, he was chagrined to find that his sudden attack wasn't the most successful and he ended up stumbling forward like a dizzy hippopotamus. The girls were shocked at his sudden display of violence all the same.

"Jerry!" screamed his sister.

"You want a piece of me, Dorknose?" Nancy raised up her far more practiced fists.

"Stop calling me Dorknose! I can't believe I trusted you!"

"Jerry, calm down," urged Gail.

"Oh, right, take her side! You always let her pick on me! I hate you! I hate you both!"

"Jerry!" cried Gail.

Sobbing hysterically, Jerry ran out into the endless corridors and platforms surrounding them, to be swallowed up by the wooden monstrosity that had become the central focal point of their lives.

"Let the crybaby go," said Nancy. "What use is he anyway?"

"Jerry's right, Nancy! You've been mean to him our whole lives! Why are you always so negative?! Why do you have to put him and everyone else down to make yourself happy?!"

"I . . . that's not—"

"You know, I bet he's right and you did tell Dr. Fell about Jerry's plan. You probably couldn't stand the thought of my brother saving the day! Can't have him upstage you for even one second, can you?"

"What, you're turning on me now too? Fine! Go run to your little crybaby brother! What do I care!"

"I hate you!"

"I hate you too!"

"I hate you more!"

"I hate you even more!"

As one, the girls marched off in different directions, each more furious than the other.

From high atop the castle walls, Dr. Fell smiled.

Chapter 16

The Mandatory Assembly of Dr. Fell

AN OPPRESSIVE SILENCE HUNG over the bus stop the next morning.

True, it hadn't been a very chatty place of late, since all the children of Hardscrabble Street—as well as those from Vexington Avenue, Von Burden Lane, Turnabout Road, and every other street, avenue, road, lane, circle, drive, boulevard, or way in a twenty-five-mile radius of Killimore Hill—spent their mornings on Dr. Fell's playground. But on this morning it was particularly quiet. This was because Gail, Nancy, and Jerry were each making a very determined effort not to speak to one another. Since they were the only three standing at the bus stop, their silence was deafening.

The morning's moratorium on conversation had actually begun the day before, after each member of the trio had stormed off with injured feelings:

Jerry was angry at Nancy for ruining his plan.

Nancy was angry at Gail for betraying her.

Gail was angry at Jerry for being too stubborn to let her apologize when she'd gotten home from the playground.

Nancy was angry at Jerry for accusing her of wanting to help Dr. Fell.

Jerry was angry at Gail for taking Nancy's side over his all the time.

Gail was angry at Nancy for being so mean to her brother.

There was a lot of anger going around.

When the bus arrived, Jerry sat down in the very front row, Gail sat right in the middle of the bus, and Nancy sat in the very back. Having been the only three at the bus stop, they sat for a moment in an otherwise empty bus—the physical distance between them echoing the emotional distance. Soon enough the rest of the kids climbed aboard (or at least as many as could rip themselves away from the playground), and the friends were just three more students on their way to school.

It was unfortunate that Gail, Nancy, and Jerry refused to speak to one another throughout the morning as well as at lunch, because each of them was witness to an alarming incident that the others would have benefited from being made aware of.

It would have been good for Gail and Nancy to know that Mrs. Wealthini took a poll in her classroom asking how many of her students had yet to visit Dr. Fell and that Jerry was the only one who raised his hand.

It would have been good for Nancy and Jerry to know that Gail saw fourth graders Daniel Dazzleford and Owen Heftybucks take a shaving kit into the boys' bathroom to deal with their facial stubble.

It would have been good for Jerry and Gail to know that Nancy overheard Lindsey Brackentwig tell Gabby Plaugestein that she planned to break her leg that afternoon at Dr. Fell's playground.

But rather than pool their knowledge and delve deeper into the mystery of Dr. Fell together, they remained three solitary islands of skepticism in an ocean of Dr. Fell worship. Which is why when Assistant Principal Richman suddenly announced that a school-wide, mandatory assembly was starting, none of the three suspected anything out of the ordinary.

Nor did they worry when the entire student body of McKinley Grant Fillmore Elementary School filed into the gymnasium to find physical education teacher Judy Moneyman standing alone in the center, waiting for students to settle down.

They thought nothing of it when Mrs. Moneyman announced that the afternoon's assembly was on a new healthy-body initiative, because physical education teacher Judy Moneyman often doubled as government-mandated health teacher Judy Moneyman.

It was when Mrs. Moneyman began talking about the sudden rash of injuries being sustained by the students that

Gail, Nancy, and Jerry perked up. And it was when a large number of parents, including Stephanie Bloom and Cecilia Pinkblossom, entered the gymnasium that they began to realize something was up.

"As your government-mandated health teacher, I felt it was important for me to design and implement a new healthy-body initiative in light of the growing number of serious injuries occurring within the student body of McKinley Grant Fillmore Elementary School," began Mrs. Moneyman. "The administrators and staff of McKinley Grant Fillmore Elementary School want only the best for our students, and a childhood filled with the repeated breaking of bones and the suffering of multiple concussions is not, on the whole, a rewarding one."

All around her, the students of McKinley Grant Fillmore Elementary School nodded their bandaged heads in agreement, with many glancing down at arms or wrists in plaster casts or legs or ankles splinted in place.

"Your parents are here today as a show of support for our new program, and they have promised to do all they can to help enforce our methods," continued Mrs. Moneyman. The parents lined up behind her all nodded enthusiastically.

At a gesture from Mrs. Moneyman, Assistant Principal Richman wheeled a large blackboard onto the stage beside her. The board was currently covered by a white sheet, and Assistant Principal Richman grabbed the edge of the sheet in preparation for whipping it off in a dramatic reveal. Once he was ready, he smoothed down his Darth Vader tie and gave Mrs. Moneyman the thumbs-up.

"Our new healthy-body initiative, which we call the New Healthy-Body Initiative, consists of three main steps," said Mrs. Moneyman, building up to the climax of the assembly. "Assistant Principal Richman? Will you please reveal the three steps of the New Healthy-Body Initiative?"

With a practiced flourish, Assistant Principal Richman swept the white sheet from the board, revealing the three steps of the New Healthy-Body Initiative.

Gail, Nancy, and Jerry immediately turned as white as the sheet that had just been removed.

"Step One!" cried Mrs. Moneyman. "If you are ever seriously injured or see another child seriously injured, you must find Dr. Fell as soon as possible. If he is not directly in front of you, you may need to search the playground for him or even go and knock on his front door."

The audience cheered. Gail dropped her head in defeat.

"Step Two!" cried Mrs. Moneyman. "Once Dr. Fell has administered to your serious injury, you must not return to play on the playground for at least one hour, unless you are feeling better."

The audience grumbled a little at this, but gave it a mild cheer just the same. Jerry's jaw dropped to the floor.

"Step Three!" cried Mrs. Moneyman. "To ensure the health of our students, all children attending McKinley Grant Fillmore Elementary School are required to visit Dr. Fell for a regular physical examination at least once a month."

The audience cheered louder than before. Nancy nearly threw up in her mouth.

"Excuse me! Excuse me! I have a problem with this!"

The cheering came to a sudden halt and all eyes turned to PTA Co-President Candice Gloomfellow, who had interrupted the celebration.

"Candy, what are you doing?" asked PTA Co-President Martha Doomburg.

PTA Co-President Candice Gloomfellow ignored her partner and plunged on. "Why should our kids see Dr. Fell on a monthly basis? That makes no sense!"

Gail, Nancy, and Jerry each felt a spark of hope flutter deep within. Was it possible there was an adult who had not yet fallen prey to the spell of Dr. Fell?

"I would feel much better if those visits were instead conducted weekly," finished PTA Co-President Candice Gloomfellow, snuffing out the children's sparks of hope.

The audience erupted into an even louder cheer as this new suggestion took hold. Mrs. Moneyman finally raised her hands for silence.

"Your concern is noted, PTA Co-President Candice Gloomfellow," she said. "But I just don't know if Dr. Fell has the capacity to see every child in the school on a weekly basis. He is, after all, only one man."

The observation that Dr. Fell was only one man brought forth a smattering of boos, which Mrs. Moneyman was able to silence with another raising of her hands.

"However," she continued, "far be it from me to judge the abilities of Dr. Fell. Why don't we ask the man himself? I give you Dr. Fell!"

The cheering rose to a decibel level unheard within the gymnasium before or since as Dr. Fell stepped out from behind the crowd of parents and bounded onto the stage carrying his black bag with the white bone handle, his purple top hat waggling back and forth. He greeted his fawning throng with a simple wave and his trademark beaming smile, letting their adulation rain down upon him. Graced with his actual presence, a number of people—both adults and children—found themselves absently muttering, "What a nice man is Dr. Fell."

In three different sections of the gymnasium, Gail's, Nancy's, and Jerry's bodies all went ice-cold.

"A supremely pleasant good afternoon to you all," he began, setting his bag down next to him. "While most certainly a monumental undertaking of herculean proportions, I must acknowledge with devout humility the exceeding wisdom in the paramount proposal currently before the floor. Though full implementation may indeed tax my aged bones beyond their capacity and leave me winded and worn, I acquiesce to the prevailing desires of the general consensus."

The cheering went silent as every single person in the room struggled to understand just what had been said. Finally, Dr. Fell cleared his throat.

"What I mean to say is . . . I'll do it."

And the cheering began once again.

Amidst the jubilation, Assistant Principal Richman stepped forward to shake the hand of Dr. Fell. "The children, staff, and parents of McKinley Grant Fillmore Elementary School are forever in your debt, Dr. Fell," he said.

"I am just doing my part to ensure the good health of

these children, who have become so dear to me," replied Dr. Fell with modesty.

Mrs. Moneyman approached carrying a large, heavy file folder. "Here are the private medical records of every child attending our school," she said, handing the folder to Dr. Fell.

"Most excellent," stated Dr. Fell, taking the offered folder and quickly flipping through the pages. "Yes. Yes. Saw him just last week. Yes. She was by yesterday. Yes. Yes. Ah!"

He thumped his forefinger down on a page and looked up, eyes alive with hunger.

"Here is a boy who has not yet graced my office. I should most definitely see him straight away. In fact, I shall personally escort him directly to my office from this very assembly."

The room hushed itself silent. Every child but three leaned forward to learn the identity of the lucky child who would be receiving such personal attention from Dr. Fell. Every child but three prayed that their name would pass from Dr. Fell's lips. Every child but three inwardly sighed in disappointment knowing they had already visited Dr. Fell and therefore could not be the child to whom he was referring.

Because every child but one had already been inside the office of Dr. Fell.

"Could someone," asked Dr. Fell, "please point out to me a young man by the name of . . . Jerry Bloom?"

Chapter 17

The True Terror Triggered by Dr. Fell

HEADS TURNED. VOICES WHISPERED. Shoulders shrugged.

Then Corey Avaricio turned to ask Britney Greedburg if she knew who this Jerry Bloom kid was. Britney wasn't sure, but she thought it might be the kid sitting between them on the bench.

His identity uncovered, Jerry quickly found himself propelled down the steps without actually being aware of moving his body. When the sea of students parted and spat him out onto the gymnasium floor, Jerry fell under the scrutiny of intense jealousy. Nearly every child present would have cut off his or her right arm to trade places with Jerry (certain that Dr. Fell would simply reattach the arm during the appointment anyway).

Of course, Jerry did not share his classmates' enthusiasm for all things Dr. Fell. Thus, while hundreds of children and adults assumed he must be boiling over with joy, Jerry was, in fact, utterly terrified. That his face did not show this terror was due only to the fact that his face was not, currently, capable of showing any emotion at all, being frozen in shock as it was.

Jerry desperately wished he had his sister with him to save him from his fate. Or even Nancy. Perhaps had they been by his side, he would have been able to wiggle out of this unwanted honor. Nancy could make up some story about how Jerry couldn't possibly see Dr. Fell today, and Gail would earnestly point out the need for Jerry to stay in school or some such rule Jerry's sudden departure would break.

But they weren't there. Jerry was alone.

Actually, he very quickly learned that he wasn't alone, which was even worse. Coming out of the pack of parents was his mother, Stephanie Bloom, bursting with pride like a mama shark after her baby has gouged and ripped open its first kill. She rushed to his side and immediately began fussing with his hair.

"I'm so sorry!" she began, again giving Jerry hope that an adult was on to the truth. But of course his mother shattered that hope with her very next sentence. "I don't know how I went this long without scheduling an appointment for you with Dr. Fell! You must think I'm a horrible mother!"

He didn't bother to contradict her. There seemed to be no point.

"Ah, young Mr. Bloom," purred Dr. Fell as he noiselessly slid between mother and son. "I am honored to be given this opportunity to attend to your physical, mental, and emotional well-being."

Dr. Fell wrapped the clammy-but-firm fingers of one hand around Jerry's arm, his surprisingly strong grip subtly closing the door on any possible escape. Jerry looked to his mother for help but knew right away that she was too far under the spell to intervene.

"I want to thank all of you for attending this mandatory assembly," barked Assistant Principal Richman, addressing the remaining audience. "Everyone can go back to their classrooms. Parents? Thank you for coming and supporting the New Healthy-Body Initiative. I'm sure with your help, it's going to be a huge success."

Dismissed, people began filing out of the room in an orderly fashion.

"Come, my child," said Dr. Fell, smiling down at Jerry and picking up the black bag with the white bone handle with his free hand. "Let us see to your health."

Like a child being led resignedly to a dinner of lima beans and chopped beets, Jerry walked out of the gymnasium with Dr. Fell, honestly wondering if he would ever return.

Though she had been frozen in terror during most of Jerry's ordeal, seeing him marched to his doom snapped Gail into action. Suddenly all the reasons she was angry with him

melted away, and she tore through the mass of obedient children on her way to the floor, shouting, "Wait! Stop! Mom! Stop them!"

Stephanie Bloom either did not hear her daughter or did not want to hear; and by the time Gail had shoved her way out of the crowd, Jerry and Dr. Fell were gone.

"Mom! You've got to stop him!"

"What, dear?" asked her mother politely.

"You can't let Dr. Fell take Jerry!"

"Now, now, no need to be greedy, Gail," said her mother. "You already had an appointment with Dr. Fell. It's your brother's turn. But don't worry, I'll set up weekly follow-up visits for you when I get home."

"I—I—!" began Gail. But the sheer weight of having to disagree with her mother proved overwhelming, and she could do nothing but watch as Stephanie Bloom walked away. To add insult to injury, Gail was pretty sure she heard her mother mumble, "What a nice man is Dr. Fell" before leaving the gymnasium.

And then the giant room was empty.

Gail fought back tears as she thought about her poor brother in the clutches of Dr. Fell. He'd zap him into a Dr. Fell zombie, sure, but Gail had a hunch—a nasty, uncomfortable, miserable, awful hunch—that this visit, this appointment, would involve much more than that. She couldn't say why, exactly, but every fiber in her being tingled in alarm. Jerry was in danger.

"Dorknose is in serious trouble."

Gail didn't turn around, so Nancy walked around to face her.

"Isn't he?" she finished.

The friends faced off, each with her respective chip high on her shoulders. The anger from the day before still smoldered, hot from the twisted bonds that can be forged only from true friendship.

"What do you care?" asked Gail finally.

Nancy bit back each of the many nasty retorts that fell over themselves in her mind in their race to be used. Gail's comment stung, but Nancy's realization that it was a reasonable question stung even more.

"I care . . . ," she began, searching for the right way to say what she wanted to say. "I care because . . . I care because he's my friend."

Gail's breath caught in her throat. Nancy continued.

"I care because nobody deserves to be swallowed up by Dr. Fell, not even a total dorknose. I care because the three of us for some reason are the only three people in this entire town who are able to ward off his spell. I care because I've known your brother for practically his whole life. I care because you are my best friend and I have no idea why I've been so angry at you all day and I can't stand not talking to you and I think it's up to you and me to save Jerry."

It was as if a dam had ruptured. Gail was instantly weeping, and Nancy grabbed her friend, held her tight, and wept right along with her.

After a few moments and a seriously good cry for both of

them, Gail lifted herself out of Nancy's embrace and wiped her eyes dry with the back of her hand.

"He's going to do something bad to my brother. I can feel it."

"I know."

"Nobody is going to do anything about it."

"We are."

Gail's eyes widened in frustration. "What can we do? He's taken him back to his house. We won't get home from school for another couple of hours, and by then it could be too late. And it's too far away to run over there."

"We'll ride bikes."

"What bikes? Mine's back in my garage."

Nancy puffed out her chest, confident. This was her area of expertise. "I didn't say we'd ride *our* bikes."

Ten minutes later, Gail and Nancy had borrowed (Gail made Nancy promise they'd give them back when they were done) two of the many bicycles ridden to school and improperly locked up that day by the students of McKinley Grant Fillmore Elementary School. The school's bike racks could accommodate maybe ten bikes, total, so by the time the twenty-third or twenty-fourth kid arrived each morning, there were bikes chained to trees, fence posts, traffic signs, and whatever else was available. The two Nancy managed to borrow had been chained to a fire hydrant, and it had been no work at all to simply lift the chain up over the top of the hydrant to liberate them.

As the two girls pedaled furiously toward Hardscrabble Street, Gail prayed they wouldn't be too late to stop

Dr. Fell from doing something horrible—and horribly permanent—to her little brother. Just what that might be she tried not to imagine, but each passing moment brought up worse and worse fears, until by the time they were halfway there, Gail had convinced herself that Jerry's very life was at stake.

Chapter 18

Jerry's Appointment with Dr. Fell

Despite the abundance of terror that began coursing through his veins the moment Dr. Fell placed his surprisingly strong, unsurprisingly ice-cold hand on his shoulder, Jerry couldn't help but be mildly intrigued in the back of his mind at the idea of riding home with Dr. Fell. This was entirely due to the fact that to this point Jerry had never seen, nor known anyone who had seen, Dr. Fell in a vehicle of any kind. He had literally walked into their lives one day. And aside from the large moving vans, not a single car or truck or motorcycle or skateboard or jet pack had ever been seen at his house.

As Dr. Fell marched him out of the gymnasium and

toward the certain doom that awaited him, Jerry struggled to guess just how, exactly, the two of them would be traveling back to the once-empty house at the end of Hardscrabble Street. Was there a magical portal shimmering in the school parking lot through which they would step? Would Dr. Fell strap Jerry to the back of a demonic beast that would bound away the miles at an impossible pace? Would they take the bus?

After blinking through the harsh glare of the midday sun upon exiting the gymnasium and seeing neither a slobbering dragon preparing to take flight nor a sleek black hearse waiting for them in the parking lot, Jerry found the courage to ask, "How are we getting back to your house?"

"Oh, my inquisitive little urchin. It is such a lovely day that I rather thought a sturdy and effortless constitutional was in order."

Seeing Jerry scrunch up his face in an attempt to make better sense of his words, Dr. Fell continued, "What I mean to say is—"

"We're walking?" interrupted Jerry.

The faintest of sighs escaped from Dr. Fell's lips—the only sign of his irritation at being interrupted. "Quite," he said. "It is but a short distance, after all."

But Jerry, who lived four houses down from Dr. Fell, knew perfectly well it was not a short distance. McKinley Grant Fillmore Elementary School was easily a couple of miles from Hardscrabble Street. It would take almost an hour to get there by foot. Realizing this, Jerry was at once dismayed and elated—dismayed at the thought of walking next to Dr. Fell for that long, but elated at the thought that his sister might get home before them, and could maybe come up with a rescue plan.

"I must admit, my fine young whippersnapper, that of my three would-be troublemakers, you have been the most impressively obstinate." He turned Jerry by the shoulder to the left and led him down a back alley behind the school. "When your sister seemed her chipper old self a few short days after our appointment, I put it down to bad luck. When the Pinkblossom girl heard my song for less than a single afternoon, I realized I was up against a true adversary."

Jerry grew alarmed, both at Dr. Fell's odd change of tone and at the fact that they were no longer on the main road. "This isn't the way to Hardscrabble Street," he said.

"I happen to be privy to a most fortuitous shortcut," remarked Dr. Fell, turning Jerry left around another corner of the building before continuing with his original narrative. "I must admit, good man Bloom, it had never occurred to me that my play structure would need to fall under the whimsical zoning ordinances of this fine community in which I have found myself. When informed of your rather ingenious plan, I was forced to take immediate steps. Steps that caused me not an insignificant amount of hassle. This way, please."

Dr. Fell's clawlike grip holding fast to Jerry's shoulder, he roughly directed the boy in a third left turn around the corner of the building into an even darker, smaller alleyway.

By now, Jerry was convinced they were not headed back to Hardscrabble Street, and he feared the worst. "Where are we going?" he asked, voice trembling.

"Home, of course," answered Dr. Fell. "We are nearly there."

"But we're nowhere near Hardscrabble Street!" pointed out Jerry, panic's tendrils wrapping themselves around his soul.

"Oh?" said Dr. Fell, highly amused with himself. He once again turned Jerry to the left, guiding his pliant victim around yet another corner of the same building. Jerry stopped cold.

He blinked. He rubbed his eyes. He stared. He was sure they had just turned left four times around the corners of one single building, which ought to have meant that they were more or less back where they'd started. Except they weren't.

They were in the middle of Dr. Fell's playground.

"Ah," said Dr. Fell matter-of-factly. As if traveling two miles in less than five minutes while walking at a leisurely pace were nothing out of the ordinary. "Here we are, then. Come along."

His voice and tone were polite and jovial, but his manner was anything but. Dr. Fell's hold on Jerry's arm tightened to the point where his long, jagged fingernails dug into the boy's skin—drawing small trickles of blood—as he tugged his newest patient out of the maze, up onto his porch, and into his lair.

Having listened in detail to both his sister and Nancy describing their experiences in this odd, ominous room, Jerry had thought he'd be prepared for his first actual visit. He was not.

The moment Dr. Fell's heavy front door thundered shut,

Jerry was practically blinded by the overabundance of purple assaulting his pupils. The room was so incredibly purple that for a moment, Dr. Fell's purple top hat disappeared into the background and it looked as though his head had simply been sliced off in a neat line at the very top.

"I would play the proper host and suggest that you recline leisurely upon my luxurious sofa while promising to be but a moment in preparation for your examination, but we both know you shall not be undergoing an examination this afternoon," said Dr. Fell grimly.

He sauntered toward the dark, stout oak door, on which hung a grim poster of two dead cats wearing ballet shoes, and yanked it open with a frightening show of brute strength. "I shall return momentarily," he said, stepping through the dark portal into the mysterious room, the interior of which remained shrouded in secrecy.

Not believing his luck, Jerry turned and ran to the front door. He was frozen for an instant at the sight of a disturbing portrait of four small, dead kittens lying together in a lump hanging on the inside of the door, but he averted his eyes and tried the handle.

The handle did not budge. The door would not open.

The fear within him rising second by second, Jerry turned and took in the room again, this time trying to look past the purple. His reward for this herculean effort was a panoramic view of dozens upon dozens of photographs of cats, most of them dead or dying, some rotting into skeletons. He recalled his sister describing these pictures but didn't remember them being painted in his mind as so overly grim.

Perhaps the most gruesome of the images adorning the walls was the portrait over the fireplace of an ancient cat stuffed into the costume of a clown. Its skin had worn thin and bare, with the poor thing's colorful insides peeking through in spots. Yet what made it utterly horrible was the fact that rather than seeming dead, the feline depicted seemed very much alive. And it did not look happy.

"Why, young Jerry, I am surprised at you," said Dr. Fell, reentering the room from the shockingly dark darkness visible beyond the dark, stout oak door supposedly leading to the examination room. "Surely you have discovered the impossibility of reopening my front door by now. I would rather have thought you would already be hard at work searching for another form of egress."

"What's in that room?" asked Jerry, pointing behind Dr. Fell at the splash of utter darkness still visible through the crack of the very slightly open, dark, stout oak door. "It's not an examination room."

"How remarkably astute you are, my dear, sweet urchin. No, it is not, in fact, an examination room. As I am not, in fact, a licensed medical practitioner. But I assume you were already aware of that particular fact."

"I'd guessed as much," answered Jerry. He backed away from Dr. Fell, who stalked forward with a truly unpleasant pleasantness about him. Jerry's legs bumped against the end of the couch, and he quickly caught himself before he could fall to the floor.

"Do be careful, Jerry," hummed Dr. Fell. "Although I suppose if you were to accidentally become injured—even gravely injured—we could most certainly take care of whatever boo-boo you imposed upon yourself. I am so very practiced at remedying childhood traumas, as I would hope has been made abundantly clear."

Though his eight-year-old body shook with terror, something instinctual ignited the fight-or-flight reflex within. Jerry quickly reached down to a plate of rotten apples sitting on a side table next to the purple couch, grabbed one in his hand, and threw it with all his might at Dr. Fell—

—who plucked it out of the air without batting an eye and proceeded to take a single, repulsive bite, all the while staring at his prey.

"Really, Jerry," said Dr. Fell after swallowing his bite. "Do you think to harm me with a piece of fruit?"

"I wish I had something heavier to throw at you," responded Jerry, quite shocked at his sudden bravery.

"Yes. I do not doubt that for a second." And then Dr. Fell leaped forward before Jerry could move and took the boy gently by the neck, smiling down into a face filled with tears. "Tell me, my fresh-faced urchin, would you like to meet my assistant?"

Chapter 19

The Lair of Dr. Fell

GAIL HOPPED OFF HER bike and let it crash to the ground next to the play structure of Dr. Fell. Running faster than she had ever run, she flew over the few yards of dry, withered grass onto the porch and bounded toward the front door. Just before she could reach out and grab the handle, however, Nancy rode her borrowed bicycle right on up onto the porch and skidded to a halt directly in front of her frantic friend.

"Get out of my way!" screamed Gail.

"Are you crazy?" asked Nancy. "You're just going to barge in there like Meaty Gluttonsen crashing a birthday celebration?"

Gail frowned, a smidgen of doubt crossing her face.

Matthew "Meaty" Gluttonsen was a very large (students were supposed to call him big boned) third grader who always seemed to shove his way into the classroom when cake, cupcakes, or other delicious forms of baked goods were being served—even if he was not, in fact, a member of that class.

"Jerry's in there!" Gail finally protested.

"Yeah, and marching into a trap is totally going to help him!" snapped Nancy. "Think, Gail! Dr. Fell knows we're going to come after your brother. He may be evil, but he's not stupid. If you open that door, who knows what'll be waiting for you. And even if there's nothing there, what do you think you'll find? An empty purple room and a big wooden door that we both know you won't be able to open."

"I have to do something!"

"Yes, *we* do have to do something. But we have to be smart about it." Nancy climbed off her bike, guiding it with one hand while leading Gail down off the porch with the other. "We need a plan of attack. We can't just make it up as we go, or we'll be playing into the hands of Dr. Fell."

They retreated to the outskirts of the play structure, automatically filtering out the cheers of joy coming from those few lucky children who had managed to play hooky from school for the day. Leaving her bike to crash to the ground, Nancy brought Gail over to a small operating room–like section of the structure and sat her down on the wooden examination table. "So hurry up and plan something," grumbled Gail, eyes continually drawn to the creepy once-vacant house standing just yards away.

"I am, I am," said Nancy, sitting down next to her friend. "What we need is an advantage."

"Like what?"

"I don't know. Something we can use that he won't have planned for. Something that gives us a leg up on him."

The two girls sat in silence for a moment, as each did her best to come up with something, anything, they could use.

"We could get our parents to help?" suggested Gail. Nancy shook her head.

"What about a disguise? Like, I could knock on his door pretending to be a traveling salesman or something?" suggested Nancy. Gail shook her head.

"Something from our exorcism room in your basement?" suggested Gail. Nancy shook her head.

"Does your mom or dad have a . . . a gun? At home?" suggested Nancy timidly. Gail shook her head. Nancy breathed a sigh of relief.

Suddenly Gail sat straight up with a start, her eyes wide as they stared off into nothing and a faint smile forming on her lips.

"You've got something," said Nancy.

"I know what we have over Dr. Fell," announced Gail.

"What? Tell me!"

Gail twisted around and flashed a look of triumph at her friend. "We were here first."

Every single child and almost every single adult on Hardscrabble Street, Vexington Avenue, Von Burden Lane, and Turnabout Road (Old Lady Witherton could not be bothered) knew there were many different ways to get into the large brick house at the end of Hardscrabble Street, which had been empty for a generation. It had occurred to Gail, however, that one person who might not be aware of the multiple points of entry was the individual who had so recently purchased the property.

She and Nancy set out to test this hypothesis.

It turned out that Dr. Fell was not quite the ignorant dupe they'd hoped. He had boarded up the broken kitchen window, nailed shut the loose board in the side of the house that had marked the opening to the secret passage through the walls into the living room, and at some point managed to fill the basement air vent with cement. He had even, in what Nancy admitted was a stroke of inspiration, found and sealed the tiny crawl space that ran from under the back porch into the basement's unused water heater.

"Huh," said Nancy.

"Huh," said Gail.

Refusing to give up, the girls quickly scaled the central pillar on the east side of the porch up to one of the many second-floor balconies to try their luck above the ground floor.

They struck pay dirt.

Not only were the rusty hinges on the window leading to one of the upstairs bathrooms still completely unattached to the wall, so the entire window could be easily pulled away, but the lock on the door leading from the master bedroom to the balcony was still nonexistent, the window air conditioner in one of the other upstairs bedrooms could still be simply shoved back inside the room, creating an opening, and the massive hole in the broken-down wall on the west side of the house had yet to be fixed.

"It's like he's never even been upstairs," commented Gail.

"Maybe he hasn't," said Nancy.

After some discussion, the two friends chose to enter the house through the huge open hole in the wall, mostly because doing so required little more than bending down and stepping through. They found themselves exactly where they expected to find themselves and exactly where they'd found themselves after stepping through that very same hole hundreds of times before—in a big closet. The closet door having long since broken off, Nancy and Gail peered cautiously into the long-deserted hallway.

Nothing had changed. The broken closet door still lay on the floor in front of them, the broken light fixture still dangled from the ceiling, a broken clock on the wall still said 4:37. The only differences between when they had regularly roamed this hallway and now were the extra layers of dust over everything and the larger number of cobwebs strewn about the place.

"You know, I really don't think he's been up here at all," said Gail.

"Which means your brother isn't up here either," agreed Nancy.

She inched out of the closet and started down the hallway, with Gail right behind her. Sunlight filtered through the crumbling brickwork of the house, causing the girls to cast a faint grid of shadows along the wall as they crept forward past empty rooms that had in times past housed secret, international spy organizations, Greek heroes, comic-book characters, zoo animals, and more.

They were just approaching the head of the infamous Stairway of Death when Gail suddenly grabbed Nancy's arm, stopping her.

"Watch out!" she cried in a strong whisper.

"What? What are—" began Nancy before remembering. "Oh, right."

And she carefully stepped over the two squeaky floorboards that every child on Hardscrabble Street, Vexington Avenue, Von Burden Lane, and Turnabout Road knew to avoid.

"Can't believe I almost forgot that," said Nancy. "Thanks."

What neither one of them mentioned was just how nervous Nancy would have to be to forget about the squeaky floorboards in the second-floor hallway.

Stepping over the boards in question, they reached the top of the Stairway of Death and peered down into darkness. The Stairway of Death had been so named not because any child had tumbled down to an unnatural end (though the stairs were certainly steep enough and rickety enough and awkwardly spaced enough to cause such an unfortunate outcome), but rather because so many children had for so many years shoved their cars, trucks, dolls, action figures (which were, to be honest, dolls for boys), stuffed animals, and—on one memorable occasion—a large, dusty bookcase down them in fits of glee. These episodes of youthful destruction had more often than not resulted in broken toys, ripped seams, shattered glass, and—on one miraculous occasion—a shockingly undamaged bookcase.

In short, the Stairway of Death was where unwanted treasures were sent to die.

Gail and Nancy stared down the dangerous stairway feeling something very much like fear. They should have been looking into the brightly lit main parlor of the house, which included a large number of windows as well as the front door. Instead, they looked down into a pitch-black nothing, which most definitely should not have been there.

"Shouldn't the big purple room be down there?" asked Gail.

"Yes . . . ," began Nancy, "but now that I think about it, I don't recall seeing this stairway when I visited Dr. Fell."

"Now that you mention it, neither do I," said Gail, frowning. "But the front door should be right there."

A moment of silence assaulted them as they tried to understand this latest mystery.

"Huh," said Gail.

"Huh," said Nancy.

Confronted with their first truly unexpected find, the girls felt the confidence that had lured them into the house drip away from them.

"Is there any other way down to the first floor?" asked Gail, who knew perfectly well there wasn't.

"No," answered Nancy anyway.

"All right then," breathed Gail. "Come on. Jerry's down there."

She gingerly placed her left foot on the first step and hesitated a moment, waiting for something truly awful to happen. When it didn't, she shifted her weight and placed her right foot on the second step. Again, nothing happened. After a quick look back up at Nancy and the filtered sunlight of the second floor, Gail swallowed her fear and walked down, step by step, into the waiting void.

After five steps of what every child knew was a nineteen-step stairway, Gail couldn't see her feet. So she held on to the railing and carefully slid her feet forward until she reached the edge, then probed downward until her foot found the next step. After ten steps she could no longer see the railing to which she clung. After fifteen steps she literally couldn't see her hand in front of her face. After eighteen steps she just closed her eyes—the darkness somehow more manageable when it was by choice. After twenty steps, however, she fell into full panic mode, because she knew as well as any child on Hardscrabble Street, Vexington Avenue, Von Burden Lane, or Turnabout Road that the Stairway of Death had only nineteen steps.

"Nancy!" she whispered. "Where are you?"

"Like I have any idea!" whispered Nancy right back. "I can't see a thing!"

"Nancy! I'm on step number twenty!"

"That's . . . that's impossible!" Nancy's voice shook with fear and, in so doing, sent Gail over the edge into terror. Nancy was her rock, the one person who wasn't scared of anything. To hear Nancy tremble with horror froze Gail in her steps.

"What do I do?" she pleaded. "Nancy, do I keep going?"

"There are only nineteen steps on these stairs!"

"I'm on step number twenty! And it keeps going!"

By now, both girls stood motionless on their respective steps, surrounded by a darkness that almost felt material. Their eyes strained to pick up any faint glimmer, any single speck of light.

"Nancy?" pleaded Gail once again, leaning on her rock.

But her rock had no good answer.

"I don't . . . I don't know, Gail. I'm . . . I'm scared."

Gail could hear Nancy deflate a few steps above her and drop to her knees. She imagined her brave friend clutching the handrail in desperation, her whole body shaking.

Just like that, Gail knew it was her turn to be the rock.

"Nancy! Nancy, listen. I'm going to . . . I'm going to keep going," she said, trying to sound confident. "Jerry's somewhere down there, and it's up to us to save him."

Nancy nodded her agreement, unable to vocalize. Of course, as they were both smothered in darkness, her nodding went unseen. Still, Gail understood her friend's response all the same.

Standing straight and holding tightly to the handrail, Gail gingerly let her feet sink down, first to step number twenty-one, then step number twenty-two, and then step number twenty-three. Three more steps that should not have been there, that should not have existed. As she descended, Gail fell into a rhythm of sliding one foot to the edge of the step, sliding her hand forward on the railing, then clenching her jaw and lowering her other foot to the next step. Again and again she did this, each time expecting it would be the last. Yet the steps continued to creep by. Twenty-eight . . . thirty-four . . . forty-one.

Her body jerked to a stop on step forty-six, and she leaned forward, straining her eyes. There was something at the edge of her vision. A soft, green, ominous glow.

"I see light!" she hissed back at Nancy, who—still huddled more than thirty steps above—could just barely hear her.

"Light? Are you sure?"

Gail crept down two more impossible steps to be sure, and the glow deepened, becoming more distinct, more real.

"Yes! There's something down here!"

Emboldened by the possibility of reaching the end of the stairwell, she quickened her pace. Each step brought the quivering green glow more into focus, until finally, at step number sixty-five, Gail's foot landed on a rough, moist dirt floor bathed in a sickly pale-green light that seemed to come from everywhere and nowhere all at once.

"I'm at the bottom!" she called back up the stairs, although whether or not Nancy could hear her was uncertain. Nevertheless, Gail inched her way forward into the chamber, taking in the rock walls from which ugly tree roots protruded like gnarled fingers reaching out for her. The underground world was moist and humid, yet chillingly cold, and her slightly squishy steps echoed back at her as she advanced forward.

Every nerve in her body begged for Gail to turn and flee back up the stairs, but something else—something unidentifiable—pulled her forward. After a few feet, she discovered what that unidentifiable magnet was.

Her brother.

Chapter 20

In the Clutches of Dr. Fell

"JERRY?" WHISPERED GAIL.

Her brother did not reply.

At first she thought he was simply standing up against the back wall, but as she came closer, she noticed first that his feet were not touching the ground, second that his eyes were closed, and third that he was wrapped up in hundreds of thin white threads as if he were a fly trussed up by a spider to be saved for a future meal.

"Jerry!" She raced to her brother's side, eyes wide with horror. The strings wrapped around his body, binding him tight, were incredibly thin and disturbingly sticky. Gail quickly began pulling them apart in a frantic rush. "Hold on, Jerry. Hold on!"

The vague suggestion of movement behind her froze Gail to the spot. She twisted around for a look but saw only blackness.

"Nancy?" she whispered. There was no reply. Yet someone was there, she was sure of it.

Or something.

Holding her breath, Gail shuffled half a step toward whoever—or whatever—was hiding in the dark void just out of sight. Suddenly another sound, much closer and much more identifiable, caught her attention—the solid thud of heavy footsteps marching down wooden stairs.

Except they weren't marching down the impossibly long Stairway of Death. Instead, they were approaching what she now saw was a stout oak door not far from where Jerry hung immobilized. Gail fought down a rising panic as the sound of the footsteps arrived at the door and was replaced by the sound of a key fumbling in a lock. At first glance, she had nowhere to hide. The Stairway of Death lay somewhere in the darkness behind her—but so did whatever was back there moving around. As she heard the key twisting in the lock, she took a desperate chance and ran toward her brother, ducking behind him and pressing herself as far back against the wall as possible just as the door swung open.

Dr. Fell bounced through the doorway with a happy little skip, the sour green glow of the room casting him in its putrid light. Ducking down, he deftly removed his purple top hat with a vaudevillian flourish and spread his arms wide.

"A supremely pleasant good evening to you, my dear," he announced seemingly to the room at large. "My sincerest apologies for barging in on you in such an impolite manner, but it simply could not be helped. I give you my sincere word, however, that our appointment will take but a moment, and then I shall leave you here so that you may continue to wallow in darkness to your heart's content."

He twirled his top hat around his fingers as he spoke, ever the performer.

Doing her best to melt into a tiny crevice in the rock wall behind her brother, Gail momentarily wondered if Dr. Fell was talking to her. She wasn't sure how he could have known she was down here, but with everything else she'd seen and heard in the past few weeks, she couldn't discount the possibility. However, a few more moments and it became apparent that the good doctor was talking to someone else—someone hiding in the darkness.

"Oh, come now." Dr. Fell pouted. "Let us not be difficult. I know you tire of this chore, but I assure you we near our errand's end. Soon, very soon indeed, our task will be complete and I shall return you to the nightmares from whence you came. You have my solemn word. Now, if you don't mind . . ."

And Dr. Fell held his hand out toward the darkness, clutching something that even in the unnatural, mystical gloom of the basement caught Gail by surprise. A glass.

Now she was seriously confused.

Her confusion grew to terror when the something that had been slinking around in the darkness moved into the light—bringing the darkness along with it. Exactly what it was—arm, tentacle, shadow—Gail would never know. It reached out tentatively, as if afraid of the light, until the very tip hovered just above Dr. Fell's outstretched glass. Then, slowly, a pulsing goop oozed down into the receptacle. Though she was too far away and the room was too dim to see clearly, Gail knew beyond a shadow of a doubt that this was the source of the odd yellow liquid Dr. Fell never seemed to be without.

After releasing only a few small drops, the appendage withdrew into the black of the nether regions of the chamber. Dr. Fell frowned as he peered down into his glass.

"This is hardly an adequate amount for my habitual needs," he said. "Have you fallen ill or forgotten to properly nourish yourself?"

He turned and spied Jerry, hanging helpless in the threads. "Have you begun healing this one? I gave him very specific injuries upon which I assumed you would administer your talent."

He walked over to Jerry with a patient ease, and Gail held her breath, praying she could remain hidden. Reaching the boy, Dr. Fell examined him with a practiced eye, spinning him around where he hung. As he spun, Gail had to stifle a gasp upon seeing her brother's knees bruised and scraped.

"He is still injured!" growled Dr. Fell, turning once again to face the darkness. "You have barely touched him!"

The horror coursing through Gail's veins at the thought of whatever was out there touching her brother became magnified as a heavy, raspy voice sounding like two large stones sliding over one another came from the void.

"Tastes . . . funny."

"Indeed. I warned you that would be the case," chastised Dr. Fell. "This one belongs to that cursed trio of cherubs to whom I made the mistake of introducing myself before releasing you from your cocoon. Like the two girls you found so distasteful earlier, his first impression of me was made without the benefit of your particular charms, which as we've learned over the years make them less palatable to you. Nevertheless, you must feed on him."

"Not . . . hungry." The voice was softer now, as if slinking away into farther recesses of its underground lair.

"You must feed! This"—Dr. Fell waved the nearly empty glass at the darkness—"is not acceptable! The boy's injuries would take three weeks to fully heal. I want those three weeks! Take them from him!"

"So . . . tired." The hoarse voice was almost a whisper now.

"I know how exhaustion plagues your very existence in this realm, but we are so close, my friend!" Dr. Fell again hopped to Jerry's side, gesturing toward him as if the boy were on display in a department store. "I promise you, suck out three measly weeks from this boy, and combined with what I have stored upstairs, I shall have enough to fully recapture my youth. Then we can leave this wretched town once and for all."

In the silence that followed, Gail felt certain the thumping of her heart would give her away. Yet Dr. Fell remained rigid, staring into the darkness. Awaiting a response.

Finally, the entity gave a weary sigh. "Not . . . hungry," it repeated. "Must . . . digest."

Dr. Fell took in a breath and stood straight, coming to a decision.

"So be it," he said. "As it happens, there are preparations I must oversee before our departure. I shall return within the hour."

He spun on his heels and exited through the stout oak door. Gail remained frozen as she listened to the key rattle in the lock, followed by the heavy footsteps of Dr. Fell bounding up the stairs. Once she could no more hear the doctor's steps, Gail slowly eased out of her nook and peered past her trussed-up brother into the darkness.

What sort of horrific monster was tucked away back there in the darkness?

"I just about peed my pants there; how about you?"

Gail jumped, startled, as Nancy appeared out of the sickly green shadows along the wall opposite the door through which Dr. Fell had just disappeared.

"Whoa!" cried Nancy, hands out in the universal sign for "calm down." "Relax, it's me."

"Relax?" asked Gail, shaking violently. "Relax?"

"OK, good point," agreed Nancy. "Panic. But do it quietly. I don't want to disturb that whatever-the-heck-it-is back there."

Gail fought the urge to scream. "I thought you were on the Stairway of Death."

"I followed you down. I was about to come over and help you unwrap poor Jerry here when Dr. Fell showed up. So I ducked back behind that pile of—"

She turned to point and suddenly stopped, which made

it painfully obvious that Nancy had not realized exactly what it was she had been hiding behind.

Even looking at it now, neither girl was able to accurately describe it. It appeared to be, for all the world, nothing less than a pile of childhood pain. There were scabs, yes, but also bruises, scrapes, and lacerations. Broken bones and twisted ankles. Sprained fingers and skinned knees. All the injuries of childhood lay clumped together, tossed into a single pile. There were worse things tucked away in there as well. Shattered elbows. Punctured eyes. Cracked skulls.

The agony of Death.

Seeing this unimaginable collection of misery brought tears to the girls' eyes. Gail wiped her face clear and turned back to her brother, even more motivated than before to set him free.

"Not Jerry," she said simply, rushing to his side and tearing threads off his body. Nancy soon joined her, and together the two made short work of his bindings. At length, he dropped to the floor, and Gail knelt beside him while Nancy removed the final strands of his bondage.

"Jerry? Jerry, wake up. Wake up!"

Gail gently slapped his cheeks and shook his arms. After a moment, a low moan escaped his lips and his eyelids began to flutter.

"Jerry!" Gail helped her brother to sit up.

"Wha . . . wher . . . whurumeye? Where—?"

"Don't try to talk," said Gail. "We're here. Nancy and I are here. You're in Dr. Fell's house, but we're going to get you home. Can you stand?"

Nancy and Gail lifted the wobbly Jerry to his feet. The young boy leaned on his sister and friend a moment before he found his footing. He opened his eyes and blinked away the exhaustion.

"It's dark," he said.

"We're in the unfinished basement," offered Nancy. "You know. Where Hannah Festerworth has always said the previous owners kept their young boy locked away."

"Oh," said Jerry, who didn't recall ever talking to Hannah Festerworth before in his life. In fact, as far as Jerry knew, the house's unfinished basement was where the previous owners had held dark cult meetings worshipping a big dirt god named Goor. Or at least that's what Zachary Fallowmold had said.

"How do you feel? Are you hurt?" asked Gail. "Are you OK?"

"I'm . . . I'm fine," answered Jerry. "Well, no. I'm not fine. I feel dizzy. And very tired. And . . . sticky?" He gingerly felt all over his body, around which the thin webbing had been wrapped. "Why am I sticky?"

"Long story," said Nancy. "We need to leave. Before that . . . that thing comes back for you."

"What thing?"

"You don't want to know."

"How do we get out of here?" asked Gail.

"We climb right back up the . . . ," began Nancy, before stopping herself. "No. No, we don't."

Climbing down the Stairway of Death in complete darkness had been hard enough, but now that they knew something . . . evil . . . brooded in the shadows, there was no way either girl would set foot back in the void of darkness on the other side of the chamber.

Gail quickly ran to the door used by Dr. Fell, only to find it locked. "We can't get out this way either," she said.

"We're trapped?" asked Nancy.

Gail peered into the darkness in the direction of the Stairway of Death, then shuddered at the memory of the creepy limb that had thrust its way into the light. She turned to her friend and brother and nodded, face contorted with anxiety.

"Wait. Wait a sec. Hold on," mumbled Jerry as the cloud fogging his brain slowly lifted. "You said we're in the unfinished basement, right?"

The girls nodded.

"Then what about the laundry chute?"

Chapter 21

Escape from Dr. Fell

GAIL'S AND NANCY'S FACES lit up.

"The laundry chute!" cried Gail.

"Duh!" agreed Nancy. "Why didn't I think of that?"

"Because you're a dorknose," teased Jerry.

"OK. If that's the basement stairs," said Gail, pointing to the door used by Dr. Fell, "then the laundry chute should be . . ." She swung her arm around and pointed to a spot on the wall not far from where she'd hidden from Dr. Fell.

Nancy ran over, waving the few remaining strands of webbing hanging from the ceiling out of her face. It took a moment in the dim, greenish light, but she soon found the old chute, which hundreds of kids had slid down from the second-floor master bedroom. She quickly lifted the rusty metal flap—wincing as it protested with a loud squeak—and stuck her head inside.

"It's clear," she informed them. "I can see a sliver of light at the top."

"OK, OK," said Gail. "You go up first, Nancy. Then Jerry, you go. I'll follow."

The order decided, Nancy pulled herself up into the chute to begin her climb. The chute was just wide enough for a child to shimmy through as long as they didn't have a problem with tight spaces.

Nancy wasn't about to admit it, but she had a problem with tight spaces. To this point in her life it had not proven to be much of an inconvenience, and it had certainly added an extra element to her desire to stay away from Dr. Fell's play structure, but suddenly finding herself compressed into the rather tiny dimensions of the laundry chute allowed this long-dormant fear to rear its ugly head. That being said, she responded as best she could.

Which is to say she froze.

"Nancy?" asked Gail, waiting to shove her brother into the chute behind her best friend.

Nancy's body was ready to receive the signals from the brain that would make it climb, but the brain was otherwise occupied. From her vantage point of being crammed into the passage, all she was able to do was emit a very high-pitched whine.

"Nancy? What's going on? Are you all right?"

Nancy was pretty sure that she was not all right. The fear slinking through her veins was of a kind she had rarely before known, matching or surpassing the fear she had felt earlier both while descending the ink-black Stairway of Death and while hearing the raspy wheeze of the . . . thing . . . that called this unfinished basement home.

Today had been a scary day.

"Nancy, please! Go!"

Facing a childhood fear can be tremendously difficult, particularly if you are a child. Luckily, Nancy had spent enough time laughing danger and trouble in the face that she was able to momentarily separate herself from the instinctual fear that kept her frozen in place.

Move it, Nancy, she ordered herself. *You can do this.*

No, I cannot do this, answered Nancy's claustrophobia. *I'm sort of frozen in fear right now.*

Snap out of it! cried Nancy. *You've been in this chute a dozen times before.*

Dropping down into the basement, reminded the claustrophobia. *That lasts all of three seconds and doesn't require us to do anything but scream.*

Good point, admitted Nancy.

The internal conversation stalled, Nancy might have remained packed into the bottom of the laundry chute for another hour or two had not a raspy, wheezy, and altogether evil voice suddenly echoed through the chamber.

"Ready . . . to eat. . . ."

Gail gasped at the unwelcome reminder of the fourth

individual currently down in the unfinished basement of Dr. Fell's home. "Nancy!" she cried. "It's awake!"

That was all Nancy needed. Shoving her phobia to the side, she squirmed and squeezed her way up, using the walls of the chute as leverage. Inch by inch she climbed, determined to get out of this house of horrors.

When Nancy's feet dangled a few feet above the opening of the chute, Gail helped Jerry climb in. Though still groggy from his captivity, he made quick work of the climb (having actually done it a number of times before) and was soon pushing up against Nancy's feet, urging her on.

Back in the chamber, Gail found herself biting her fingernails to the nub as she waited for the bottleneck in the laundry chute to open up. Behind her she heard a sickly flapping sound coming from the darkness, as if something very wet was slapping the ground and pulling itself forward.

"Hungry . . ."

"Hurry!" shouted Gail, too overcome with fear to worry about keeping her voice down.

In the chute, Nancy was painstakingly forcing herself upward. She could see the top of the chute directly ahead, could reach out with one hand and just scrape the bottom of the poorly sealed laundry lid with her fingernails. Beneath her, Jerry did what he could to help, letting the girl who not long ago had been his archnemesis literally step on his head when she needed to.

"Meal . . . leaving . . . ?"

The change in the creature's tone caused Gail to swivel her head around and look behind her.

She would spend the rest of her life wishing she hadn't.

What she saw was darkness itself. Some unformed thing had slithered out into the dim green glow, bringing the shadows with it. Though she could not see the creature, she was able to make out the horrible outline of its shape. Lumpy and drooping. Multiple arms or legs or tentacles. A pulsating mass that might or might not be a head. Just the shape of the thing was enough to haunt her nightmares, but what hit her in that single terrifying moment was how the blackness of night seemed to be sucked toward the being, as if lovingly covering a child from the chill.

Gail's scream gave Nancy a final burst of adrenaline, and the claustrophobic girl rocketed up the final few inches until she was able to grab hold of the top of the chute and pull herself out. She flopped to the dusty, splintered floor of the second-story master bedroom, curled into a ball, and wept. An instant later, Jerry climbed out of the chute, then immediately turned back and shouted down to his sister.

"We're clear, Gail! Get out of there!"

Gail leaped into the chute and made her way up. Her going was slower than her brother's, as she'd never shimmied up the chute before, yet faster than Nancy's, as she did not suffer from claustrophobia. Focusing on the encouraging face of her brother at the top, she was making good time until Jerry's face of encouragement turned into a face of fear.

"Behind you!" he shouted.

Suddenly Gail felt something grab her ankle. She screamed, assuming it was the creature of darkness. The next

words she heard, however, both relieved her fear and replaced it with one far worse.

"And just where do you think you are going, my dear young urchin?"

Dr. Fell's icy fingers stabbed into Gail's ankle, pulling her down. She thrust out her arms to jimmy herself inside the chute and slow her descent, but her reprieve wouldn't last long.

"My, but you have been a naughty one," droned Dr. Fell. "I do believe that steps shall need to be taken to ensure your rather prominent nose remains vacant from the affairs of others in the foreseeable future!"

Clutching Gail's ankle in his viselike grip, he pulled her slowly but surely down the shaft.

"What I mean to say is . . . it is time for you to be silenced."

He tugged hard, and Gail closed her eyes, screaming as her arms lost their grip. But just when she was certain the old man had pulled her to her doom, two strong, callused hands grabbed her arms from above, holding her in place.

"Kick him!" yelled an unrecognizable voice.

Gail did as ordered, kicking down with her free leg and getting a moment's satisfaction when she landed a solid blow on the top of the head of Dr. Fell.

"Ow!" bellowed Dr. Fell, losing his grip on Gail's ankle. The strong, callused hands immediately yanked her up and out of the laundry chute, placing her gently but firmly on her feet.

"Run, child! Run!"

Gail's heart beat in overdrive as she quickly turned to look at her savior.

It nearly stopped when she found herself looking into the eyes of a very serious, very determined, and very bothered Old Lady Witherton.

Chapter 22

The Name of Dr. Fell

"OLD LADY WITHERTON!" SHOUTED Gail.

"Go, child!" shouted Old Lady Witherton right back at her, pointing a gnarled, spotted, and surprisingly meaty finger toward the window, where Gail could see the top of Nancy's head dropping out of sight. "Skedaddle already!"

Gail ran to the window and poked her head outside, to find a large wooden ladder leaning against the side of the house. Nancy was halfway down and Jerry stood at the bottom waving her on.

"It's Old Lady Witherton!" shouted Gail, her mind refusing to accept this surprising turn of events.

"We know!" called Jerry from below. "Hurry!"

"But what's she doing here?" asked Gail.

"Saving our butts!" answered Nancy, dropping the final few feet to the ground.

"I thought she couldn't be bothered," said Gail.

Suddenly the same gnarled, spotted, and surprisingly meaty fingers grabbed Gail firmly by the shoulders, shoving her through the window and out onto the ladder. "Get the lead out, girl! Evil's a-coming!"

At Old Lady Witherton's urging, Gail quickly climbed down and joined Jerry and Nancy at the foot of the ladder.

"Where did she come from?" she asked.

"No idea!" admitted Jerry. "She's like a ghost!"

The ghost in question dropped to the ground beside them and quickly shooed her young charges away. "Don't stand there dawdling," she fired at them. "Run!"

With a sudden, horrific roar of rage coming from deep within the basement providing an extra adrenaline boost, the three terrified children and the little old lady fled from the lair of Dr. Fell faster than they had ever known themselves capable of fleeing.

Behind them, the intermittent animal-like cries were momentarily joined by angry flashes of an eerie, dim green light that seemed to seep up through the very ground itself as if struggling for freedom.

Gail, Nancy, and Jerry sat sipping hot chocolate in a brightly lit living room crammed full with puffy chairs, frilly lampshades, big dusty books, and cats. Doilies were everywhere, and there didn't seem to be an inch of fabric in the entire room that didn't end in some form of fancy old-lady lace.

Old Lady Witherton stood in the center of the room, arms crossed, waiting patiently for the three children to regain their senses.

Each of the children had questions. Each of the children was desperate for explanations. Each of the children sat quietly on the same couch sipping their hot chocolate and letting their eyes wander about the room.

Finally, Nancy took an unnecessarily loud sip and set her cup and saucer down on a lace coaster. "All right," she announced. "Lay it on us, lady."

"Nancy!" snapped Gail. "Don't be rude."

"I just been waiting for y'all to finish yer cocoa," said Old Lady Witherton. "Come with me. We got a lot to talk about."

She led the children out of the Room of the Doilies, through a very cluttered kitchen, and down a narrow corridor ending at a wooden door. Opening the door revealed a rickety wooden stairway leading down into darkness.

"Not another basement," complained Gail.

"Oh, hush," said Old Lady Witherton, flipping a light switch outside the door and bathing the stairs with light. "I promise there ain't no monsters lurking down there waiting to suck out your soul. Not in my house."

She tramped down the steps and stopped at the bottom, hitting another light switch. The children followed her down to find an ordinary, medium-sized, finished basement filled with power tools and badminton sets, beach chairs and luggage, a water heater, and a washer and dryer. In fact, had it not been for the worktable piled high with knives, swords, axes, flails, morning stars, and other assorted instruments of medieval combat, it could have been any other basement in any other home on Hardscrabble Street, Vexington Avenue, Von Burden Lane, or Turnabout Road.

"Now then," said Old Lady Witherton, welcoming the children into her basement. "I'm sure you have questions."

"You bet we do," said Nancy. "Like, who are you? Why do you have all these weapons down here? How did you know we were at Dr. Fell's? How did you know we were in danger? Why'd you come and save us?"

"What was that thing in his basement?" added Gail, joining in. "What's Dr. Fell been doing to all the kids? Why did Dr. Fell come here? How come everybody is in love with him?"

"How come you're not in love with him?" continued Nancy. "What does Dr. Fell want? Where did he come from? What was that creepy light down there?"

"Who is Dr. Fell?" asked Jerry.

The girls turned to look back at the youngest member of their trio.

"That, my poor little dovelings, may be the most important question of them all." Old Lady Witherton crossed the room to the worktable and reached up to a long shelf, hanging on the wall above it. She grabbed the shelf's lone occupant—a large, dusty, hardback book—and pulled it out.

Then she coughed from the eruption of dust that followed the book from the shelf.

"Are you all right?" asked Gail, who hoped their sudden savior was not about to hack up a lung.

After a couple more coughs, Old Lady Witherton pounded herself on the chest and turned back to face the children. "Sorry about that. I ain't big on housekeeping down here."

She handed the book to the children. Nancy took it, then started to drop it once Old Lady Witherton let go. Gail quickly helped her, and the two of them held the ridiculously heavy book together.

"You'll find your answer in there," said Old Lady Witherton.

"Which one?" asked Nancy.

"His," responded Old Lady Witherton, jabbing a finger at Jerry, who peeked over his sister's shoulder at the large volume.

The children looked around for a place to sit. Seeing none, and with the surface of the worktable overflowing with sharp instruments of maiming that hailed from the Middle Ages, they struggled with the weighty book and ultimately came up with a system where the two girls held the book in their arms while Jerry turned the massive pages one by one. The cover seemed to creak as it yawned wide in Gail's arms.

"You kids are lucky I been keepin' an eye on that house," stated Old Lady Witherton, watching them. "When I saw you girls breakin' in like that, I knew trouble was a-brewing."

"What, exactly, are we looking for in here?" Gail asked, looking up from the book.

"The man's name," replied Old Lady Witherton. She scuttled back to the table and began inspecting the various tools of death for nicks and scratches.

"His name is Dr. Fell," snapped Nancy irritably.

Old Lady Witherton raised her eyebrow while running her finger over the edge of an especially lethal-looking axe. "Young lady, there ain't never been a mommy or daddy who named their baby Doctor."

"What are you doing?" asked Jerry.

"Gonna need me some fightin' tools," answered Old Lady Witherton. "Y'all keep flipping pages. You'll find it."

Returning their attention to the book, the children widened their eyes in amazement as Jerry turned one heavy, thick page after another, venturing deeper into the mysteries of the book. Every page was covered with tiny, handwritten notes jotted down between pencil-drawn images of hideous-looking people and creatures pulled from humanity's worst nightmares. Interspersed were pictures of a tall man in black with a purple top hat, usually wearing something gold somewhere on his body.

"Old Lady Witherton—" began Gail.

"Constance, honey," interrupted Old Lady Witherton as she set down the axe and picked up a wicked-looking spiked ball dangling from the end of a chain. "My name is Constance."

"OK. Constance," continued Gail, "what is this book?"

"A history of the crimes and horrors done to the people of the world by Dr. Fell," answered Old Lady Witherton.

She punctuated her statement by swinging the chain over her head and smashing the spiked ball into the wall in front of her. The three children jumped and screamed, dropping the book.

"Oh, sorry there, little lump-muffins. Didn't mean to startle you. Just making sure everything's in working order for my assault."

The three children silently agreed to ignore that last remark and instead bent down to pick up the book. They froze, however, because the fall had jostled the right number of pages over, to reveal the very thing for which they searched. The name of Dr. Fell.

After a moment, they stood up straight, bewildered. Finally, Gail voiced what they were all thinking.

"Faustus Felonious Fell?"

"The one and only," said Old Lady Witherton, straining to pull the string tight on a crossbow she was holding.

"Should that name mean something?" asked Nancy.

"His ... name ...," grunted Old Lady Witherton as she pulled and stretched and finally snapped the string into place. "Whew! Either that string has gone and shrunk or I really am getting old. Where was I? Oh, yes. His name means everything. It's who he is. It's what he is. And it's a warning. Faustus Felonious Fell is a bad, bad man."

"We already knew that," argued Nancy.

"But do you have any idea how long he's been a bad, bad

man?" challenged Old Lady Witherton, absently swinging the crossbow in their direction. The children dropped to the ground to get out of the line of fire. "What if I told you that Dr. Fell . . . that evil, evil man . . . is well over five hundred years old?"

She was met with blank stares of disbelief from her squatting audience. Jerry looked at his sister to confirm that she'd heard the same number he had. Gail, in turn, looked at Nancy for similar confirmation.

"Five hundred?" asked Nancy for all three of them.

"At least," said Old Lady Witherton, setting the crossbow back on the table, much to the relief of the children. "I've found written mention of him as far back as 1512, but there are oral histories goin' back even further."

"But . . . how is that even possible?" asked Gail, standing back up.

"Oh my sweet, dear little dovelings. Ain't you figured out yet what it is he does?"

The children stared at her, either not understanding or, in Jerry's case, not wanting to believe.

"He steals your time," said Old Lady Witherton sadly, answering her own question.

Gail, Nancy, and Jerry shared a look of confused fear, causing Lady Witherton to sigh, swipe her arm across the worktable to clear a space, and sit down on the edge.

"I suppose it's story time," she whispered, staring down at the floor. "Gather round, my little dovelings."

Chapter 23

Constance's Appointments with Dr. Fell

"I WAS SIX YEARS old when Dr. Fell entered my life," began Old Lady Witherton. "We lived in a tiny little town in Texas on the coast of the Gulf of Mexico, where nothing ever happened. But then one day, of course, something up and happened. Something horrible. Dr. Fell came to town."

Her entire body shivered as the memory came over her. She closed her eyes a moment to let the unpleasant emotions pass before taking a deep, calming breath.

"He was just a harmless-looking old man," she continued. "Dressed as ever in his black suit and purple top hat, carrying that silly little old black doctor's bag with the white bone handle and wearing a shiny gold bracelet.

Everybody up and loved him from the start, no questions asked."

"Everybody except you, you mean," said Nancy. "You saw through him."

"Heavens, no!" exclaimed Old Lady Witherton. "I thought he was the bee's knees. He was funny and silly and always had a pocketful of candy to pass out to his 'urchins,' as he called us. Why, we'd all gather like roaches on a dung heap up and down the street for a chance to shake his hand and walk away with a sweet. When he set up shop and hung his shingle outside his door, I was first in line for a physical examination."

"Did he . . . did he build a playground?" asked Jerry.

"Well now, no. I can't say as he did. Not in so many words," answered Old Lady Witherton. "But he did give us fun-starved children a proper thrill. He went and built us a carousel."

"Carousel?" asked Nancy.

"A merry-go-round," answered Gail.

At the mention of the carousel, Old Lady Witherton's eyes glazed over and a look of pure joy crossed her face. "Oh, it was a sight," she said. "Two rows, each with a dozen of the most beautifully carved horses you ever did see. Watching them go round and round, you'd swear they were galloping along on their own. Children would swarm over them and race each other, as if the horses weren't bolted down to the floor."

"But that's silly," said Jerry. "They just went in a circle, right?"

"I suppose they must have, but it certainly didn't feel that way to us. We all had our favorites, of course. Mine was a fine white mare I named Lollipop. She was faster than the wind, and so beautiful I couldn't help but cry with joy every time I looked at her. She may have been carved from wood, but if so, it was the softest, finest wood I ever did see. I could close my eyes and imagine myself running my fingers through her mane, and I swear to you it felt real. I loved that horse. And she loved me. Which is why I was so surprised the first time she threw me off her back."

"You fell off the horse?" asked Gail.

"Weren't you listening, child? She threw me. I didn't blame her, of course. She didn't mean to. I think she got spooked by one of the other horses. But no matter. Off I sailed into the air, landing on a pile of rocks poorly located to the side of the carousel. Oh, I landed good and hard and heard a number of things break, and a part of me wondered how I could possibly still be alive. I screamed something fierce, my whole body trembling with an agony I shall never forget."

"What happened to you?" asked Jerry.

"Why, Dr. Fell happened, of course," she answered, her entire demeanor souring at the mention of his name. "In the blink of an eye he was there, gathering me up in his arms. He carried me inside his doctor's office and . . . well . . . the next thing I knew, I was all better. He gave me an extra piece of candy that day, and I fell in love with him all the more."

"That sounds familiar," noted Nancy with a frown.

"Oh, my dovelings. I told you, he's been doing this for centuries. He has his system down pat."

"How badly were you injured?" asked Gail.

"You know, I honestly don't know. Looking back, I would guess pretty bad. At least a broken leg, if not worse. But Dr. Fell worked his magic, and I climbed back up on Lollipop the very next day."

"Weren't you scared?" asked Gail.

"Are any of your friends scared of playing on his foul, evil play structure?" challenged Old Lady Witherton, pointing one of her fingers at Gail's chest. "Even when they've broken an arm the day before?"

The three kids all shook their heads with understanding.

"Then, of course, Lollipop threw me back into that rock pile the very next day. It never occurred to me that maybe there was something wrong with the carousel. I simply wasn't holding on tight enough. So after Dr. Fell once again brought me inside, fixed me up good, and gave me an extra piece of candy, I vowed nothing would make me let go of Lollipop's luscious mane. I gripped it as tight as a schoolboy gripping his lunch money when he walks by the school bully. Nothing was going to make me let go."

"She threw you again, didn't she?" said Nancy.

"Of course she did! And the next day and the next. For thirteen long days I repeated this pattern. Each time becoming more obsessed, more focused, more determined than ever to hold on."

"What about your parents?" asked Jerry. "Your friends? Didn't anybody say anything?"

"Have any grown-ups said anything about his playground?" responded Old Lady Witherton. "This is what he does, my little dovelings. He casts his spell over a

neighborhood, and everybody falls into line. I wasn't the only child being thrown from the carousel into the rock pile, of course. All of my friends were going through the same thing in one form or another. But I daresay none of them were as swept up in his clutches as I was. I was special."

"Why?" asked Gail.

Old Lady Witherton buried her face in her hands for a moment, and the three children worried they'd somehow upset the poor woman. Finally, she looked up and dried her eyes with the backs of her hands. "Because it takes my body a long time to heal from injury. I suffer from diabetes. When I break a bone, it might take twice as long for me to fully heal as it would for somebody else."

"Oh, wow," breathed Jerry.

"What? I don't get it," snapped Nancy.

"Dr. Fell steals your time," explained Jerry. "You get a fat lip that would normally take a week to heal; he heals you instantly but takes that week from your life. So if he found someone who would give him twice as much time for the same injury . . ."

"You become his favorite patient," finished Old Lady Witherton sadly. "And so I was. And when it was all over? After thirteen days of breaking bone after bone, only to be magically healed? I looked in the mirror and saw not the six-year-old girl I'd been a week before, but a young woman in her late teens. Dr. Fell had stolen my childhood."

Gail, Nancy, and Jerry sat in utter shock at this revelation.

"I was born sixty-one years ago," said Old Lady Witherton. "But I don't look a day under seventy-five, do I?"

The children could do little more than blink at the tragic woman before them. Perhaps knowing they needed time to digest everything, Old Lady Witherton stood and began shoving various weapons into her belt, preparing for battle.

"And now you're going to get your revenge?" asked Nancy carefully.

Old Lady Witherton whirled around, eyes wide and indignant. "Revenge? That man must be stopped, my dovelings! Do you know what happened when he left my little seaside town, my dovelings? Because he did leave. Just up and walked away, a sprightly young man skipping his way down the street and out of our lives. Skipping with the energy of youth he'd stolen from me and all my friends. Do you want to know what happens to a community when Dr. Fell is through with it?"

She snatched up the crossbow, whirled, and shot a bolt past the children straight through three beach chairs hanging one behind another on the wall.

"The community dies," she said. "Everyone wakes up from whatever daze they've been under and sees the horror of what he's left behind. Parents, suddenly realizing they've been urging their children to injure themselves, divorce in shame. Kids who suddenly find themselves two or three or, in my case, over ten physical years older than they were when he arrived try to adjust, run away, or simply go insane. Everybody blames everybody else, lifelong friends become enemies, people move away, and a once-happy neighborhood is left in ruins."

The enormity of the situation chilled the three friends

to their very bones. Each of them, however, found the inner strength to stand, determined. Ready to do what had to be done.

"All right then," said Gail, speaking for them all. "How do we stop him?"

It was all Old Lady Witherton could do not to laugh.

"We? Oh, my sweet dovelings, thank you so much for your bravery, but this is between me and Dr. Fell. He's evil, ruthless, and vile, and I will handle him alone."

She immediately raised her hands to quiet the sudden arguments arising from her pronouncement. "I didn't save you from his clutches just to turn around and let you walk right back into danger," she said. "When I first learned he'd arrived in town, I was sure he'd come looking for me. I was scared and I failed to warn anyone, failed to do anything while history repeated itself in front of my eyes. Well, no more. If he really has come to suck up more of my time, he's welcome to try. I don't have all that much left for him to take anyway. But you three? You've your whole lives ahead of you. Go on home. Go home and forget you ever heard of Dr. Fell."

Chapter 24

The Call of Dr. Fell

Gail, Nancy, and Jerry continued to object, but Old Lady Witherton could not be swayed. She led them out of her house on Turnabout Lane, pointed them in the direction of their homes near the top of Hardscrabble Street, gave them a stern warning about trying to follow her, then set off through the surrounding backyards toward the lair of Dr. Fell and whatever fate awaited her there.

The children walked home in silence, each lost in their own thoughts. The revelations from Old Lady Witherton had put them in a somber mood, and each of them secretly wanted to put the whole matter behind them, if only for a moment.

Determined to honor their promise and not interfere with Old Lady Witherton's attack on Dr. Fell, they kept to the streets, taking the long way home rather than cutting through yards. So it was that five minutes later, they turned onto Hardscrabble Street and prepared to go their separate ways. Without saying a word, Nancy stepped out to cross the street and head home, when Gail stopped her.

"Do you think she'll do it?" she asked. "Do you think she'll stop him?"

Nancy paused a moment before answering, taking the time to gaze through the graying light of evening toward the large brick house at the end of Hardscrabble Street. "No," she said, finally.

"Really?" asked Gail. "And you're OK with that?"

"What can we do about it? Old Lady Witherton is right. We're just kids. Dr. Fell is . . . he's something bigger than the three of us."

"We escaped from him," reminded Gail.

"Only with her help," reminded Nancy right back. "Look, I hope I'm wrong. I hope Old Lady Witherton has what it takes to stand up to Dr. Fell and his . . . his darkness. But I'm not holding my breath."

The two friends again looked down the street at the home of Dr. Fell, each imagining Old Lady Witherton alone in that dark, unfinished basement going up against the horrible creature and/or Dr. Fell. It was not a happy imagining.

Suddenly Jerry, who Nancy and Gail had almost forgotten was there, spoke up.

"A gold bracelet."

"Huh?" asked his sister.

"When she told us her story, Lady Witherton mentioned that Dr. Fell wore a gold bracelet. I don't remember ever seeing him wear a gold bracelet."

"It was a long time ago," said Nancy.

"Yeah, I know," said Jerry. "But everything else was so much the same. The black suit. The purple top hat. The black bag with the white bone handle. Even in those pictures in the book. Always the same, and always with something gold. Why would this time be different?"

Neither of the girls had an answer. "Is it important?" asked Gail.

"I don't know," admitted Jerry. "Maybe. Maybe not."

The conversation petered out at that point. The kids all knew they should probably head home, but none of them wanted to leave the other two. They stood motionless on the street corner, at once worried and nervous and anxious. They knew there was a very strong likelihood that *something* was going to happen that evening, but they weren't sure what it would be, or if they should try to be a part of it.

Above them, the sky darkened as the last rays of the sun sank beneath the horizon, signaling the official beginning of night.

And something happened.

The streetlights all blinked on at once, of course, but that was to be expected. None of the three children so much as noticed the sudden illumination of dozens of pale bulbs—none of which was strong enough to fight back the oppressive darkness descending onto the neighborhood. What did draw their attention, however, was the sudden opening of every single front door on Hardscrabble Street. This was quickly followed by every single man, woman, and child stepping out of his or her home and turning as one to walk down the street toward the home of Dr. Fell.

"What's going on?" asked Nancy, despite seeing events unfold before her eyes.

"Where is everyone going?" asked Gail, despite the sudden crowd's obvious destination.

"Why does everyone look like zombies?" asked Jerry, despite knowing full well the power of the spell cast by Dr. Fell.

"Mom! Dad!" cried Gail, breaking into a run to catch up to Jonathan and Stephanie Bloom, who were mindlessly strolling down the sidewalk. Nancy and Jerry quickly followed.

The first thing Gail noticed when she caught up with her parents was the whisk clutched in Stephanie Bloom's hand. The second thing she noticed was the frying pan carried by her father. The third thing was the look of blissful ignorance etched on the faces of both of her parents. "Mom!" she said, stepping in front of her mother. "What are you doing?"

Stephanie Bloom looked down at her daughter, and for half a second, Gail wasn't even sure her own mother recognized her. But then the dazed woman blinked her eyes, smiled, and addressed her daughter. "Dr. Fell is in trouble," she said without stopping. "We need to rally around him.

You and your brother need to run in and grab one of the heavier skillets or rolling pins and join us."

"I . . . but—but . . . ," stammered Gail, her need to obey her parents fighting her need to stop Dr. Fell.

"Go on," said her dazed father. "Be a good girl."

Gail took a step back, and Jerry could see his sister start to give in. But then she clenched her fists and jumped directly in front of her parents.

"No! We have to stop Dr. Fell. He's evil!"

"Evil?" asked Stephanie Bloom curiously. "No, I don't think so. Not at all. What a nice man is Dr. Fell."

Gail was shocked into silence at this reply. She stood rooted to the spot as her mother and father calmly continued down the street with their kitchen tools.

"Is that a whisk?" asked Nancy.

"Dr. Fell has sent out some weird telepathic call," said Gail. "They're all running to his defense."

"Walking," corrected Jerry.

"Old Lady Witherton!" cried Gail. "We have to warn her!"

"How?" asked Nancy.

"We could . . . I mean . . . we . . ." Gail struggled for an idea. "What if we . . . well, how about—"

She was suddenly interrupted by a deafening explosion that knocked all three children—as well as everyone walking toward Dr. Fell's—to the ground. A deep boom reverberated from the far end of the street, and a ball of eerie green fire rolled up out of the large brick house at the end of Hardscrabble Street and into the sky.

"Nancy? Jerry? Are you all right?" called Gail as she forced herself up onto her wobbly feet.

"I've got a bruised butt, if that matters," said Nancy. "But otherwise I'm fine."

"It's happening, guys," said Jerry, eyes wide with panic. "It's actually happening!"

"What's happening?" asked Nancy.

"The end! This is the end! If we don't do something now, Dr. Fell will finish what he's doing here and disappear, and our school, our street, our friends, our family—they'll all be ruined!"

Gail and Nancy wiped dust and debris out of their eyes and looked hopelessly at each other.

"We can't just stand here and do nothing!" pleaded Jerry.

"Jerry's right, Nancy," said Gail. "Whatever is going on at the end of the street, it can't be good. Old Lady Witherton is only one woman—she can't defeat Dr. Fell all by herself."

"We're just kids!" argued Nancy. "He's five hundred years old and has a creepy monster of darkness working for him. What can we do?"

"It doesn't matter, because we're the only ones who can do it," said Gail. "Everybody else is under his spell. If our community is going to be saved, it's up to us."

She thrust out her hand toward Nancy and Jerry. Jerry immediately placed his atop his sister's. The Bloom children stared at Nancy Pinkblossom, waiting.

Finally, Nancy thrust her hand out to meet the other two

in solidarity. "I can't let you and Dorknose look brave while I run away like a coward," she said.

The three children gave one another a confident nod, then turned and ran as fast as they could toward the chaos that was quickly encompassing the world of Dr. Fell.

Chapter 25

The Playground of Dr. Fell

AT FIRST, THE CHILDREN felt weird as they ran past neighbor after neighbor walking calmly toward Dr. Fell's house armed with an assortment of kitchen implements. None of those they passed took any notice of them, focused as they were on answering the freaky telepathic call that was luring them down the street. Stephanie and Jonathan Bloom were oblivious to their children's passing, and Cecilia Pinkblossom barely gave her daughter a glance as Nancy rushed by. Nancy paused only long enough to identify the turkey baster her mother held in her hands.

After quickly weaving their way through the mesmerized

residents of Hardscrabble Street, the children came suddenly in sight of the home of Dr. Fell and discovered a very serious problem with their off-the-cuff plan to run into the house, find Old Lady Witherton, and help her defeat Dr. Fell.

The house was no longer there.

The eerie green ball of flame that had lit up the night sky moments before had left nothing but rubble in its wake, and the three children stood momentarily confused by the lack of a building into which they could dash.

"Maybe she won?" asked Gail.

"Don't you think if she'd won, we wouldn't still be dealing with the march of the living brainless?" responded Nancy, thumbing behind her at the wide circle of neighborhood residents slowly but surely advancing on the site of the explosion.

"Well, she can't have lost yet either," said Gail. "Or else Dr. Fell would've called everybody off."

"They're underground," said Jerry. "In the chamber of that . . . thing."

"So how do we get down there?" asked Nancy.

But just as she said it, she realized the answer. As did Gail and Jerry. All three turned to look at the massive, untouched, impossible play structure standing ominously in the darkness. Slight shivers shimmied down each of their spines as they all independently got the odd sensation that as much as they were looking at the play structure, it was looking right back at them.

"I think Christian Gloomfellow said there was a dungeon

section over there behind the scale model of Notre Dame," said Jerry as they entered the labyrinthine play structure.

"No," corrected Nancy, climbing up a rope ladder. "That's a World War One trench. I remember Gabby Plaugestein saying the dungeon was right in front of the alien spaceship."

"Wait," called out Gail. "I remember Albert Rottingsly saying there was a pixie bog in front of the spaceship, not a dungeon."

Jerry wormed his way through the window of a mad scientist's laboratory. "Gore Oozewuld once told me there were big sewer tunnels in the Roman section," he said. "That might be a way in."

"What about Atlantis?" asked Nancy, sliding down a fire pole into the cockpit of a stealth bomber. "Didn't Hannah Festerworth mention an Atlantis section once?"

"The tombs!" exclaimed Jerry. "I remember Bud Fetidsky talking about a series of tombs, like from Indiana Jones. I think he said they were just past the pirate ship."

Though they hated to admit it, all three children quickly realized that since they'd never spent all that much time actually playing on the play structure, they had no idea where to go or how to get there.

"Guys, this isn't working," said Gail, swinging over to a square platform that had most recently seen use as a dance stage, a kickboxing arena, and a floor for gymnastic routines. "We can't just run off in different directions. We need to stick together."

Nancy climbed across the wings of the stealth bomber,

jumped over to a swaying bridge, then hopped over the back of a wooden dragon to join Gail on the platform. "You're right," she said. "If we go up against Dr. Fell one by one, we don't stand a chance."

Jerry popped his head up from beneath the platform. "So we need a plan of attack," he said as the two girls reached down and hauled him up onto the platform. "A way to get through this labyrinth and find him."

"And Old Lady Witherton," added Gail quietly.

"All right." Nancy paced along the edge of the platform. "We've obviously all heard different things about this place, so we can't trust anything we've been told. Where does that leave us?"

"We have to just search," said Gail. "Together."

A muffled roar suddenly reverberated from somewhere deep within the playground, causing all three to jump.

"What was that?" asked Nancy.

"You know very well what that was," answered Gail.

Nancy nodded, trying not to shake from fear.

"I don't think we have time to do a complete search," warned Jerry. "All our zombie-like friends and family will be here any minute, and once that happens, it's game over. We need to be smart."

"So be smart," snapped Nancy. "That's your thing, isn't it?"

Jerry opened his mouth to shoot off a retort but then realized that in her own way, Nancy had just complimented him. "OK, OK. True or false. The playground seems bigger almost every day."

"True," answered Gail.

"True or false. Some things in here actually seem to move around so they're never in the same place."

"True," answered Nancy.

"True or false. Wherever that cavern of his is, it was here from the very beginning. He needed a place to keep his . . . creature."

"True," answered Gail and Nancy together.

"So what does that tell us?" asked Jerry.

The girls just looked at him, so he answered his own question. "It tells us that it isn't moving around. That it's probably under the middle of the playground. And that the middle of the playground probably hasn't been moving around. So all we have to do is figure out what part of this thing has stayed the same the whole time it's been here."

It took maybe half a second, but then all three of them turned and peered out and up into the mass of towers and spires and skyscrapers that dotted the roof of the play structure. And in the midst of these—higher than anything else—stood the mast of the pirate ship.

After wading through the swamp bog, running through the circus tent, swinging across the lava pit, and climbing over the ruins of Pompeii, Gail, Nancy, and Jerry finally arrived on the deck of the pirate ship. Jerry and Nancy quickly fanned out, searching for a trapdoor or other secret entrance, while Gail found herself drawn to a spot on the deck beneath the mighty mast, which dominated the landscape.

"Gail! Come on!" shouted Nancy. "Help us find the way in!"

"This is where that boy fell," said Gail, stopping her companions in their tracks. Silently, Nancy and Jerry walked over to join Gail in staring down at the deck.

"Leo something, wasn't it?" asked Nancy.

"Leonid Hazardfall," corrected Jerry. "That's where he died."

"That's where Dr. Fell killed him," corrected Nancy.

"Before bringing him back to life by stealing years of his life away," finished Gail. "Just like he did to Old Lady Witherton. Back when she was Young Girl Witherton. Can you even imagine?"

"Losing my childhood?" asked Nancy. "No."

"Old Lady Witherton says he's been doing this for over five hundred years," said Jerry. "Think how many childhoods he's stolen. How many lives he destroyed."

"That's why we're stopping him," announced Gail. "Not for us. It's too late for Leonid Hazardfall and Bud Fetidsky and everyone else in our neighborhood who's had years ripped away from them. But this is where it ends."

"This is where it ends," agreed Nancy.

"This is where it ends," agreed Jerry.

The three of them quietly spread out and got to work. They searched every nook and cranny of the pirate ship, climbed up every pole and mast, opened up every empty barrel. Finally, Nancy hauled aside a massive coil of rope, and there it was—a deep, dark hole leading down into an even deeper, darker nothing. The three stood around the rim of the hole, squinting and peering and trying to make out anything down there. But it was no good. It was as if light itself refused to shine into the depths of Dr. Fell's lair.

There was no need to speak. The three children nodded to one another, clasped hands, and dropped into the void.

Chapter 26

The Prisoner of Dr. Fell

THEIR FEET LANDED ON a hard dirt surface far sooner than they expected, and the children found themselves standing in a circle of pitch blackness. They remained together, holding hands and gazing all around them. The seemingly impossible fact that they could make out the walls and glow of the cavern in the distance, yet could not see the hands in front of their faces, caused their hearts to skip a beat.

"It's like we're in a spotlight of darkness," said Jerry.

"A spotdark," agreed Nancy.

"Let's get out of this," said Gail.

The three tentatively took a step, each pulling in a different direction. After a moment of blind negotiations during which time none dared release the hands they held, the others agreed to let Gail lead the way. She slowly pulled them forward, step by step, out of the darkness. After a few steps, she was able to make out the boundary of the black spot. Quickening their pace, she finally yanked herself and the others out of the oppressive circle of darkness and into the much larger cavern of mostly darkness.

"We made it," said Jerry. "We're here."

"Again," mumbled Nancy.

At first glance, the cavern seemed little changed from their adventure only a couple of hours before. The walls gave off the same eerie green glow, the horrific pile of childhood trauma was still sprawled against the wall, the door through which Dr. Fell had come and gone was again just barely visible at the far end of the room.

At second glance, however, the children all noticed something very, very different.

"Where's all the darkness?" asked Gail.

Before, more than half of the cavern had been hidden by the same physical darkness the three had just leaped into. But now, aside from the small circle of black beneath the pirate ship, the cavern was merely poorly lit. The children could even see the bottom of the impossibly long Stairway of Death sitting quietly against the wall behind them.

"Do you think maybe Old Lady Witherton won after all?" asked Jerry.

"No," said Nancy. "She didn't win."

"How do you know?" asked Jerry.

"Because she's wrapped up in the same sort of junk you

were trapped in when we found you." Nancy pointed to the far end of the cavern. The children could just make out someone in the corner, body bound tight by the odd white strands and feet dangling inches off the ground. All around the prisoner lay the various swords and axes and crossbows Old Lady Witherton had armed herself with before heading off to face Dr. Fell.

"No!" squeaked Gail, breaking into a run.

That it was Old Lady Witherton became undeniable before Gail had crossed half the distance. The old woman hung suspended in the air by the awkward webbing, her eyes and mouth open in a frozen, silent scream.

"She doesn't look any older," noticed Jerry as he arrived at his sister's side.

He was right. Trapped though she was, it was evident that Dr. Fell had not loosed his nightmare creature on her just yet. Nancy immediately began ripping the individual strands away from their neighbor. "Come on—let's get her out of there."

As Jerry joined her, Gail slowly turned in a circle, gazing all about the room. Something was wrong.

"Something is wrong," she said.

"This is Dr. Fell we're dealing with," grunted Nancy. "Lots of things are wrong."

"Where's the darkness?" asked Gail. "I don't mean the darkness. I mean . . . you know . . . the Darkness."

"Who cares? Hurry!" Nancy's attempt to clear Old Lady Witherton of the flimsy, thin wisps grew frantic, as more and more seemed to just stick right back together around the old woman the instant they'd been removed.

"No." Gail shook her head, every nerve in her body screaming out in warning. "This is wrong. This is all wrong. We have to get out of here! It's a trap!"

"I would venture to state unequivocally that our young prognosticator has shown a wisdom beyond her years in her ability to pierce the veil of my subterfuge," said a chuckling, high-pitched voice, which caused all three children to break into a sweat. "What I mean to say is . . . young Gail is right."

The children watched as a cloud of perfect darkness floated down the Stairway of Death. At the very edge of the darkness—leading it down into the cavern, as it were—marched a youthful and energetic Dr. Fell, his smile chilling the very air it touched. He approached the children and spread his arms wide in greeting.

"You cannot know how satisfying I find it to finally have the illustrious trio of do-gooders by my side as I complete the latest of my periodic episodes of rebirth," he said. "Not being greedy, I would have been content to ingest but a few more weeks of youth from young Jerry earlier today before making my departure. But now. Now I have other plans."

He came right up to the three children and tilted his abnormally long neck to peer down on them from above. Behind him, the entire cavern had been blacked out—consumed by the darkness.

"Why?" asked Gail, looking helplessly up into Dr. Fell's eyes.

The evil man cocked his head to the side, amused by the question. "Why? Not generally what one expects to hear from the condemned. Very well. Why?" His smile grew so large, it seemed to encompass his ears. "Because I can. And because you three insignificant little urchins are unable to stop me."

"Don't be so sure," said Nancy, finding an unexpected well of courage somewhere inside her. "You don't control us. We're not under your spell."

"Well now, that is quite the astute pair of observations, my temperamental lass." Dr. Fell lifted up his black bag with the white bone handle with one hand and lovingly rubbed the soft leather with the other. "It is certainly true that due entirely to my own negligence, the three of you have proven immune to my many charms. I made the unfortunate mistake of allowing you to craft a first impression of me before I had woken my servant from its cocoon. You see, my . . . friend . . . is not from here. Once awoken, it resonates, if you will, an energy of absolute love and obedience toward me. Over the years—or I suppose I should say centuries—I've learned that this energy has the odd yet fortunate effect of causing others who meet me to feel the same. Unless they have already met me. In which case, they do not generally share the communal affection for me. Luckily, I have more direct methods of control at my disposal. Allow me to demonstrate."

He snapped open his bag, and hundreds of small, almost transparent balls floated up into the air. A quick, forceful exhale from Dr. Fell sent the balls flying into the faces of the three children, who raised their hands up in a futile attempt to swat them away. The balls expanded, pulsating and shimmering with a ghostly inner light, and attached themselves all over the children's skin. As Gail, Nancy, and Jerry cried out in a mixture of fear and frustration, more and more of the slimy balls coated them, until the sheer weight of these globular invaders dragged each child down first to his or her knees, then all the way to the cold, hard floor.

"I do apologize for any discomfort caused by my little toys." Dr. Fell smirked, closing up his bag. "Normally my subjects are unconscious when they do their work. Alas, I felt a certain urgency in the situation and chose not to stand on ceremony."

Now that all three children had been subdued, the balls on their bodies began pulsating and bubbling. Out of each stretched dozens of the strange, thin white strands, which proceeded to wrap themselves around their subjects. Other strands reached toward the ceiling, and slowly but surely the children were lifted off their feet. As Dr. Fell hummed pleasantly to himself, Gail, Nancy, and Jerry were trussed and bound in a manner identical to that used for Old Lady Witherton. In what seemed like only a few quick moments, the three of them hung in a line in front of Dr. Fell, staring at their captor in horror.

"There," he murmured. "That's better. Now then, who would like to go first? Any volunteers?"

"You're a monster," said Gail, spitting the webbing out of her mouth.

"Oh, my sweet, innocent little child. You have no idea

what I am." His trademark grin wavered a moment into a look of pure hatred. Gail gasped in fright, then spent the next several seconds spitting more wispy strands out of her mouth.

"It occurs to me that we already have a patient in need of my care." Dr. Fell marched down the line, stopping in front of Jerry. "Unless I am very much mistaken, you still have a boo-boo on your knee, do you not?"

Jerry shook his head, not trusting himself to speak.

"Come now, don't be shy." Dr. Fell reached through the webbing and pulled up Jerry's pants leg until the red scrape from before was visible. "This won't hurt a bit."

He turned away to address the darkness, but then stopped and twisted his head back around. "It honestly will not hurt, in case you were curious. You will not feel a thing."

He returned his attention to the darkness behind him. "Come out, come out, wherever you are, my pet."

The children held their breath and stared, too terrified to blink. The dark void in front of them seemed to writhe and wriggle about, yet nothing appeared to answer Dr. Fell's call. At length, he frowned and tried again. "Come forth, my friend. I have need of you."

Again the darkness pulsed and slithered, yet again it refused to appear. Dr. Fell grew increasingly angry. Taking a deep breath, he lifted one hand up to his chest (though what exactly he was doing the children could not see) and called out, "Heed my summons, Fiend, or face my wrath!"

The darkness came alive, squeezing itself forward in jerks and spasms. "I . . . come . . . ," claimed the heavy, raspy voice from within the black.

"Much better," said Dr. Fell, lowering his hand. "Now then. If you would be so kind as to attend to the boy's injuries."

With a gesture toward Jerry, Dr. Fell stepped aside. At first, the children could not make anything out in the darkness. But then, bit by bit, forms took shape. Limbs or tentacles or arms or legs pulled themselves forward, as if dragging a great weight. Dim yellow pinpoints of light that might have been eyes blinked on and peered intensely at Jerry. Then, more than a shadow, the darkness itself lurched toward the young boy caught in the abominable webbing. Jerry could not scream, could not look away, could not do anything as the terrifying darkness reached out and swallowed up his knee.

"Get away from him! Leave my brother alone!" Gail thrashed about as best she could.

Jerry stared down at where his knee should have been but where he could see only a jet-black nothing. It was as if his knee had ceased to exist. Or as if it had vanished into an alternate universe.

Then the dark tentacle pulled away from Jerry and receded into the larger mass of darkness. Jerry's knee was suddenly right where it had always been. And the raw, nasty-looking scrape on his flesh was gone.

"There now. Was that really so awful?" asked Dr. Fell.

"You just stole his time," accused Nancy.

"A trifling amount," replied Dr. Fell. "How long do you suppose it would have taken for that particular injury to heal? Two days? Three? Also, if we are, indeed, being technical, it was not I who absconded with those three days. It was my . . . companion. Point of fact, I have never stolen a single moment from a single child in all my long, long history. I am not, after all, a monster."

"But you . . . you get young!" yelled Gail in frustration.

"Oh, you noticed?" Dr. Fell smiled and flexed his youthful muscles. "Yes, I can see how you might be perplexed by this puzzling conundrum. You see, the real monster at work . . . the creature that haunts the darkness . . . feeds not on time but on pain. It digests the pain of one's injury, and in so doing inadvertently digests one's time. A side dish, if you will. But as it has no use for the time it devours, it excretes it through the tips of its limbs much as your own body excretes water through your pores on a hot summer's day. The time is a waste product, nothing more. All I do is collect this waste product and ensure that all that precious time does not go to waste."

He turned back to address the darkness. "Are you ready for a full meal, my pet?" he asked.

"Not . . . hungry," came the tortured reply.

"I did not ask if you were hungry," said Dr. Fell darkly, his tone threatening.

An idea began to form in Jerry's mind.

"Now then," announced Dr. Fell, twirling back around. "I have need of a gruesome, horrific injury that would take months to heal. But what should it be? A broken leg? Cracked skull? Some hideous internal injury? Shattered vertebrae? So many choices."

"Please," whispered Gail. "Don't hurt us. Just go. You're

young again. You can disappear and no one will ever find you. You've won."

"Oh, I have most certainly won, my poor, pleading friend. But I desire to do more than just win. I want to crush you. To ensure that none ever again dare oppose me like this batty old crone." He gestured at the still form of Old Lady Witherton. "I tire of living a lie, of maintaining the facade. I want the whispers of what happened here on Hardscrabble Street to spread far and wide, so that when I next step out of the shadows a withered old man, people will line up to give me their youth willingly for fear of facing my fury!" A fire raged in his eyes as he spoke, the evil within finally breaking through the mask he so carefully cultivated.

"You really are a monster!" cried Gail.

"No!" screamed Dr. Fell, pointing behind him. "There is the monster! There is your evil! There is your creature of ultimate darkness! I am merely the one controlling it!"

Jerry's idea began to take shape.

"Since you are so very critical of my work, little Gail, I think you shall be the first to have the honor of donating your youth." Dr. Fell approached Gail, wrapped in her cocoon, and began ripping strands away from her legs. "I should think a fractured shinbone most appropriate. Those bones take a devilishly long time to heal. It would ordinarily keep you in a cast for close to a year. I will take that year."

"Leave her alone!" yelled Nancy, punching the air in front of her and partially freeing one of her arms.

"No . . . eat . . . ," moaned the voice from the darkness. "Taste . . . bad. . . ."

"You will do as I say or face the consequences!" snapped Dr. Fell.

The children were surprised to hear what sounded like whimpering coming from the black void.

Jerry's idea locked into place.

"Now, hold still, little one," growled an obviously annoyed Dr. Fell, reaching in and grabbing hold of Gail's left leg. "This is going to hurt quite a bit."

As she squirmed and wriggled in a frantic attempt to free herself from his grasp, and as Nancy continued to yell and punch in a frantic attempt to free herself from the strands of webbing, and as Dr. Fell's eyes bulged with anticipation, Jerry's idea hatched.

"His watch!" he yelled. "Go for his gold watch!"

The outburst distracted Dr. Fell, who turned his head, suddenly alarmed, just as Gail wrenched her leg free and kicked with all her might at the gold chain tucked into his suit pocket. The first kick caught Dr. Fell in the gut, knocking the breath out of him. The second hooked the chain around the tip of her foot and yanked it up and out of his pocket, sending it flying into the air.

"You brats!" screamed Dr. Fell, reaching up to catch the shiny gold watch as it soared above him.

"Nancy!" yelled Gail.

"Got it!" Nancy yelled back, ripping her arm all the way out of the webbing with a final grunt of effort. Everyone watched as the watch dropped down as if in slow motion toward the ground in front of her. Straining beyond what she would have thought possible, Nancy groped forward, making a final lunge with as much of her body as the strands wrapped around it would allow.

The watch landed in Nancy's palm with a satisfying thunk.

"Trash it!" yelled Jerry.

Dangling above the floor as she was, Nancy had few options, and she looked about desperately as Dr. Fell got to his feet and approached her, face contorted with fury. "Give that back right now!"

"The ceiling!" cried Gail.

With the menacing form of Dr. Fell less than a foot away, Nancy suddenly tilted her head and shoved her free hand up, slamming the gold pocket watch against the rocky cavern ceiling.

"No!" bellowed Dr. Fell. He flinched back a step as if it were he himself being smashed against the rock and not his pocket watch.

"Keep going!" cheered Jerry.

Nancy slammed the watch against the ceiling as hard as she could, cracking the casing a little more with every strike. Gail joined Jerry in cheering Nancy on.

One more smash and the cover of the watch broke off, revealing the glass face beneath.

"Stop! You do not know what you are doing!" wheezed Dr. Fell, his entire body suddenly shivering in fear.

And a third voice joined Gail and Jerry in urging Nancy on. A raspy, grinding, horrific voice that nevertheless sounded suddenly joyful.

"*Go!*" called out the creature of the darkness.

With one final thrust, Nancy smashed the glass face against the rock ceiling, shattering the pocket watch. Shards of glass, tiny gears, and splinters of mechanical doohickeys rained down around them, and an exultant cry of glee echoed throughout the chamber.

"Free . . . free!" bellowed the darkness.

Dr. Fell dropped to his knees and gathered as many of the pieces of his former watch as he could. "What have you done, you filthy vermin! What have you—"

He never got a chance to finish the sentence.

The mass of black swept forward and engulfed him, wrapping its tendrils around the youthful-looking man, pulling him off his feet and backward into the void. Even his screams of horror were suddenly cut off as he vanished into a vibrant blackness darker than night.

All three children closed their eyes as a bright light burst forth from deep within the nothing in front of them. For an instant, the cavern was illuminated with an intense, yellow-purple essence that threatened to blind them even through their eyelids. But then, just as instantly, the pulse of energy was gone.

Slowly, Gail opened first one eye, then the other. The cavern, while still dimly lit, was no longer black. Even the circle of utter black beneath the pirate ship was replaced by the hazy glow of star- and moonlight filtering down from above.

"What just happened?" asked Nancy.

"I think . . ." Jerry paused, hesitant to give voice to the hope welling up within him. "I think when you smashed the watch, that . . . thing . . . was free to return to its own . . . whatever. And it took Dr. Fell with it."

"Did you know that would happen?" asked Gail in awe.

Jerry shook his head, wild-eyed. "Are you kidding me?"

"Oh my heavens," murmured Old Lady Witherton, stirring in her cocoon. "You're all trapped here too. We're doomed. Dr. Fell will kill us all!"

"No, Constance," replied Gail. "I don't think Dr. Fell will ever hurt anyone again."

Chapter 27

The Legacy of Dr. Fell

After Nancy finished ripping herself free from the thin white strands, she quickly helped the others down, until all four former prisoners of Dr. Fell had their feet on solid ground once more. The large doorway through which they had seen Dr. Fell enter and exit in the past was not to be found, so Gail led the others up the Stairway of Death into the smoking ruins of what had once been the large, empty brick house at the end of Hardscrabble Street.

"Gail! Jerry!" Stephanie Bloom raced over and wrapped her children in a mammoth hug. "Thank God you're OK!"

"What in blazes just happened?" asked Jonathan Bloom.

"What was that big explosion?" asked PTA Co-President Martha Doomburg as she and a number of other neighborhood parents approached.

"Why is everybody standing around holding kitchen tools?" asked Veronica Plaugestein.

"Where did you four come from?" asked Abner Fallowmold.

"What is Old Lady Witherton doing here?" asked Sandy Gallowsbee.

"Was she bothered?" asked a slightly worried Horace Macabrador.

"Where is Dr. Fell?"

The adults all turned as one to look at little Ethel Pusster, who stepped forward and repeated her question.

"Where is Dr. Fell?"

"Dr. Fell is gone," answered Old Lady Witherton. "And good riddance to him."

Everyone opened their mouths to automatically defend Dr. Fell but found themselves suddenly seeing him in new ways.

"I always felt rushed during his appointments," muttered PTA Co-President Candice Gloomfellow.

"I don't recall ever seeing his physician's license," said Lars Oozewuld.

"What was with all those pictures of cats?" asked Sharon Rottingsly.

Everybody nodded and agreed with her on that point.

And so the people of Hardscrabble Street, as well as all

those on nearby Vexington Avenue and Von Burden Lane, and nearly all on Turnabout Road (Old Lady Witherton could not be bothered), quietly made their way back to their homes, walking down streets whose streetlights seemed to burn just a little brighter than before.

For her part, Old Lady Witherton knelt down before Gail and Jerry and Nancy (grimacing slightly as her arthritis kicked in) and clasped her hands in front of her in thanks. "You saved my life," she said. "Or what's left of it. Thank you, you dear, sweet dovelings."

The children smiled.

"Nancy? Nancy!"

Nancy looked up to find her mother rushing over to her. She stopped a good foot or two away, suddenly feeling awkward with everyone watching. Nancy smiled, closed the distance, and gave her mother a big hug.

"I love you, Mom," she said.

Cecilia Pinkblossom blushed, then wrapped her arms around her daughter. "I love you too," she said. "Honey, do you have any idea why I'm carrying the turkey baster?"

And so life slowly returned to normal. Or, at least, it found a new normal.

The whirlwind of life under the sway of Dr. Fell was over, but the damage done lived on. Leonid Hazardfall hit puberty at a surprisingly young age and developed into a star middle school and high school athlete who seemed, physically at least, to be years ahead of his peers. Other children at McKinley Grant Fillmore Elementary School, as well as those at Lincoln Adams Coolidge Elementary School, Washington Madison Hoover Elementary School, and Ford Garfield Taft Elementary School, also found themselves rushing through childhood perhaps a little faster than they would have liked. And every boy in the entire sixth grade of Southeast North Northwestern Academy had to be taught how to shave.

Those were only the more obvious, physical ramifications. As Old Lady Witherton had warned, a number of parents found themselves second-guessing their decisions or those of their spouses during the time of Dr. Fell, and sadly the bonds within more than a few families were tested.

But the more horrific examples of devastation left in the wake of Dr. Fell described by Old Lady Witherton failed to appear. Perhaps because, at the end, he had not left on his own terms, or perhaps the people living in the shadow of Killimore Hill had simply gotten lucky.

His play structure, of course, was torn down right away, with children and parents working together to disassemble the devious death trap. In less than a week, all that remained at the end of Hardscrabble Street was the burned-out husk of the old house. Even the immense basement had disappeared. There was nothing strange or sinister or remotely magical left behind. Just an empty vacant lot.

After some discussion among neighborhood parents, it was decided to build a new playground down there. Money was raised, a contractor was hired, ground was broken, and the new playground became the envy of the area. It had a climbing wall, swings, slides, a big space ball built of rope—a bunch of things for kids to climb on or over or under. It also had a very soft, sandy play surface.

It did not have a pirate ship, or a moat, or a tower, or a dungeon, or a spaceship, or the Pyramids of Giza, or a life-sized dollhouse, or ancient ruins, or a circus tent, or a zip line dangling hundreds of feet above the earth.

And that was fine.

One day a few weeks or months later, three friends sat on the bank of the tiny trickle of a stream that snaked behind Hardscrabble Street, lost in their thoughts and memories. The three children had spent many days like this, uneasily sitting together, apart from the other children, each day more unsettling than the last.

Like the other children of the neighborhood, they liked the new playground at the end of Hardscrabble Street. Like the other children of the neighborhood, they had initially played on the new playground at the end of Hardscrabble Street. Like the other children of the neighborhood, they had expected the hundreds of new, happy memories spent playing on the new playground at the end of Hardscrabble Street to replace the less pleasant ones that had been created in that same space all those weeks or months ago.

But unlike the other children of the neighborhood, these three had been unable to forget Dr. Fell.

And so as the days wore on, they were less and less inclined to be seen cavorting on the playground at the end of Hardscrabble Street. Less and less inclined to be seen playing with the other children. Less and less inclined to smile at all.

And more and more inclined to feel that something was wrong.

"I wish we didn't remember him," said Gail, and not for the first time.

"It doesn't seem fair," agreed Nancy. "Everybody else is forgetting him."

"Everybody else was under his spell," Jerry pointed out. "Maybe, since they were in a dreamlike state when he was here, they're now all sort of waking up. Like how it's harder and harder to remember a dream the farther away from it you get."

"But we weren't dreaming," said Gail. "So we remember."

"Right," agreed Jerry. "We were wide awake."

They sat a moment longer as a small leaf floated down the trickle of a stream in front of them.

"Do you really think he's dead?" asked Gail, voicing the question that was on all their minds.

"He's survived for over five hundred years, my dovelings," said a voice they all immediately recognized as belonging to Old Lady Witherton. "I promise you, he survived this."

The children looked up and found the old woman standing on the opposite shore of the tiny trickle of a stream. They shifted in place and prepared to stand, but she waved them back down as she stepped over the foot-wide brook and joined them.

"Now, now, don't get up. I just came to say good-bye," she said.

"Good-bye?" asked Gail, standing.

"You're leaving?" asked Jerry, also standing.

"I needed some time to get everything in order, but now, yes," she announced. "I'm leaving."

"Where are you going?" asked Nancy, who had already stood up.

Old Lady Witherton took a deep breath and looked up at the cloudless sky. "Out there," she said.

"You're going into space?" asked Jerry.

"No, dear. Sorry. I was being dramatic. What I mean to say is—"

"Please don't say that," said Gail.

Old Lady Witherton stopped, then nodded, understanding. "What I should have said is that I don't exactly know where I'm going. I just know it's time to go."

The children frowned and kicked absently at the dirt. "You're going after him, aren't you?" asked Gail at last.

"Oh, my sweet little dovelings. You mustn't worry about such things. You have years and years and years of life ahead of you. Don't waste it worrying about him."

"But he could come back!" cried Nancy.

"Not here, dear," Old Lady Witherton assured her. "He never returns. Only arrives. Hardscrabble Street shall not see Dr. Fell ever again."

With that, Old Lady Witherton patted each child affectionately on the head, then turned and walked back over the foot-wide trickle and off into the woods on her way back to her little house on Turnabout Road.

Just before she disappeared into the trees, Gail called out one last time. "Will we ever see him again?" she asked.

Old Lady Witherton paused a moment, then turned her neck only partly back around, so that rather than looking at the three children, she gazed down at the ground just behind her.

"I suppose that depends on whether or not you stay on Hardscrabble Street," she said.

Then she melted into the trees.

On the darkest of nights, in the darkest of back alleys, in an especially dark city, there appeared a vast darkness. The darkness was followed by a roar. The roar was followed by a bright yellow-purple light. The bright light was followed by a grunt. The grunt was followed by a thud. Then the bright yellow-purple light disappeared.

As the light retreated, a man remained behind—lying facedown in a small puddle.

The man turned his head to the side to clear his nose and mouth from the murky water and breathed in, then out, then in again. He then pulled his arms up, placed his palms square in the muck, and pushed himself to his hands and knees. A few seconds passed as the man struggled to regain his breath.

Had anyone bothered to duck down this particular dark back alley in this particularly dark city on this particularly dark night, they would have seen a handsome young man slowly gather his feet under him and stand, breathing heavily from the effort. They would have seen

this handsome young man wipe his dirty hands on his blacker-than-black suit pants. And then they would have seen this handsome young man carefully bend over and pick up a purple top hat.

"Well, that was distinctly unpleasant," they would have heard him say before he set off into the night.

But of course, nobody was there.

Acknowledgments

A huge thank-you to Ann, Phoebe, and Griffin for encouraging me, and allowing me to barricade myself upstairs from time to time to write. Thank you also to my editor, Emily Easton, for pushing me to answer some questions in the story while allowing others to remain a mystery. I am grateful to Eric Myers for believing in my work, and to Chris Grabenstein for deciding I was worth passing along to Eric in the first place. Thank you to Jerry, Judy, Abbey, Elisabeth, and Sahalie for giving me critical notes on earlier drafts—your feedback shaped this into what it has become. Finally, I am forever indebted to the late illustrator Trina Schart Hyman for taking an obscure four-line rhyme from 1680 and turning it into an illustration that inspired me to bring Dr. Fell to life.

About the Author

David Neilsen is a classically trained actor/storyteller, a journalist, and a theater/improvisation teacher. During the Halloween season, David can be found telling spooky tales to audiences of all ages, or performing one of his one-man shows based on the work of horror author H. P. Lovecraft. David lives in New York with his family. *Dr. Fell and the Playground of Doom* is his first novel.